Moira's Old Life	Moira's New Life
Chauffered limousine	Driving stick-shift for the first time in her new boss's new car—and getting a speeding ticket
Maids and laundry service	Her new dog vomiting in her new boss's new car—and not a maid in sight
A personal assistant to plan her day and look over her shoulder	A new boss to plan her day and look over her shoulder
Giving up freedom for fame and comfort	Giving up her heart—to her new boss!

There was just so much for a princess to learn about being "average"....

Dear Reader,

When Chloe Marshall met Princess Moira back in college she never dreamed they'd one day be trading places. Imagine small-town girl Chloe in a 130-room castle with a maid, a stretch limo—and a gorgeous king, hers for the asking!

And where has the real princess been all this time? Well, you're about to find out what Moira's up to with the sexiest cowboy in the west!

We hope you enjoy this fun duet from popular author Jenna McKnight! If you missed Chloe's story, you can order #719 *Princess in Denim* from the Harlequin Reader Service. U.S.: 3010 Walden Ave., Buffalo, NY 14269. Canada: P.O. Box 609, Fort Erie, Ont. L2A 5X3.

If you'd like a bookmark from Jenna McKnight, you can write her at P.O. Box 283, Grover, MO 63040, or e-mail her at Connections at the Harlequin web site at: http://www.romance.net.

Happy reading!

Debra Matteucci
Senior Editor & Editorial Coordinator
Harlequin
300 E. 42nd St.
New York, NY 10017

Cowgirl in Pearls

JENNA McKNIGHT

Harlequin Books

TORONTO • NEW YORK • LONDON
AMSTERDAM • PARIS • SYDNEY • HAMBURG
STOCKHOLM • ATHENS • TOKYO • MILAN
MADRID • WARSAW • BUDAPEST • AUCKLAND

ISBN 0-373-16724-5

COWGIRL IN PEARLS

Copyright © 1998 by Virginia Schweiss

Printed in U.S.A.

Prologue

It's hell being a princess.

Moira sat on her sumptuously cushioned chair and tried to look comfortable. She didn't mind listening to the symphony play Bach and Beethoven in the county park. She didn't mind that her attendance helped Santa Barbara raise money for any number of worthy projects.

She *did* mind that a dozen children sitting around her were licking ice-cream cones as the sun dipped lower in the sky. But *noooo,* that wouldn't be proper for a princess. Not even one that was twenty-eight and loved a scoop of anything with the word chocolate in it.

If wishes came true, she'd be more like her best friend. Chloe Marshall wouldn't let anyone tell her she couldn't eat ice cream when she wanted. Moira had tried to be like Chloe once or twice, when they'd traded places for a day here, a weekend there.

Oh, what heaven that had been! To walk to the beach alone—really *alone,* without a secretary or a bodyguard; to spend a whole day without a minute-to-minute schedule; to carry cash in her purse and shop in a real store; to be approached and talked to and treated like a real person...

To the right of the audience, a paparazzo crept along the perimeter, staying low, trying to hide his camera beneath his jacket. The paparazzi never stopped. *They* were part of the reason she couldn't enjoy ice cream along with any other average person attending this evening. *They* would catch her on film, and how would that look on the front pages? Princess Moira, in silk and sapphires and a chic broad-brimmed hat, with her tongue sticking out?

"There's one on the right side," Emma, seated beside her, said.

Moira sighed. Her personal secretary was well schooled in protecting Moira, but it wasn't enough. Emma wasn't the one who hated having her picture taken by complete strangers and splashed across front pages. One photo had been altered to show Mel Gibson's arm slung possessively around her shoulders—as if anyone would ever allow *that* to happen. Emma wasn't the one who'd had to develop evasive maneuvers.

At the last moment, as the paparazzo leaned over for what he surely hoped would be a clear shot, Moira tilted her head ever so slightly to the right. Just enough to dip her brim and ruin his shot.

"Well done," Emma said. "Though if you'd let them get a good picture once in awhile, they'd lose interest."

"Only until the next issue."

The only way to be treated like anyone else, Moira knew for a fact, was to *be* someone else. She'd done it before. Could she do it again?

In the limo on the way back to her condo, the

chauffeur and Emma safely up front on the other side of soundproof glass, Moira dialed Chloe's apartment.

"Hello?" Chloe answered groggily.

"Did I wake you? I thought you had to study all night."

"I do." Chloe's yawn was muffled. "Thanks for waking me so I could get back to it. How was the concert?"

"Same as always. Um, Chloe, I have a proposition for you."

"You want to take my exams for me?"

"Oh, yeah, I know *so* much about geology."

"What then?"

Remembering that cell phones weren't secure, Moira was suddenly unsure whether to continue. "Maybe we'd better talk in person. When can you meet me at the barn?"

Chapter One

Moira, former royal princess of Ennsway, rushed through the mountain airport, swept along in the midst of hundreds of travelers who were all taller than she and all seemed to know where they were going. It was go with the flow or get trampled. She had no idea whether she'd end up in the baggage claim area, where to pick up her dog, how to find transportation to the dude ranch, or how to explain to her new boss why she was a day late.

This was the world she wanted.

From the top of her ball cap, complete with blond ponytail swinging out the back, to the worn soles of her scruffy cowboy boots, she looked as American as apple pie. That might be a cliché to anyone born and raised in the United States, but she'd only been here sixteen years—and every last one of them spent as a visiting princess.

Until now.

"Excuse me," a man mumbled on the fly as he pushed past her.

Pleased that no one paid her any undue notice, no one bowed or curtsied, no one tried to snap her picture, Moira smiled with satisfaction and replied to the man's disappearing back. "Anytime."

At the baggage claim area, she watched carefully to see how an average American woman in Colorado reclaimed her bags. As much as she wanted to be like everyone else, the crowd was a bit overwhelming for a first-timer. It pressed in tighter, obscured her view and eventually nudged her to the back.

"Get your bags for you?" a uniformed skycap offered.

"Yes," she answered gratefully.

He held out his hand.

No man had ever offered to shake her hand before. As a royal princess, she'd always made the first move.

Or was she supposed to tip him? *Before* he got her luggage? Chloe, with whom Moira had traded places, had explained all this to her, but the rules were suddenly very fuzzy. On top of that, other than getting a little jostled in today's crowd, she'd never actually touched a man to whom she hadn't been introduced first. And they certainly hadn't touched her.

But wait, logic prevailed. *Would Chloe pay someone to do something she could do herself?*

Moira looked at the skycap's brown eyes, his impassive face, anywhere but at his hand, which was still stuck out there, palm up. "Never mind. I'll, uh, get them myself."

As the skycap shrugged and turned to someone else, relief swept over Moira. She'd prevented two mistakes with the same answer. She'd remembered to be a normal, everyday cowgirl and get her own bags, and she'd solved the dilemma of what to do with the skycap's proffered hand. Nothing.

She still wondered which would have been correct,

though, so she watched him. The next woman he approached nodded and handed over her claim tickets.

"Stupid, stupid, stupid," Moira cursed beneath her breath. Mistakes like that could expose her for what she really was. If she was going to pull off this "everyday American girl" persona, she was going to have to do better.

She successfully retrieved her three mismatched suitcases and dressage saddle, then displayed her claim tickets to prove they were hers—as if any thief in his right mind would try to steal bags so ugly and of so little value. With her saddle over one arm and the luggage balanced on a little hand cart, she was on her way to a car rental desk when she walked by a man holding a sign with her new name on it: Chloe Marshall.

She backtracked, looked him over in his tan suit and cream-colored cowboy hat, and asked, "Are you looking for me?"

"Chloe Marshall?"

She nodded and tipped the cart up on edge. She'd barely lifted her arm to give it a rest when he grabbed her hand and pumped it enthusiastically.

"Nice to meetcha. I'm Billy Bob Rydell, from Rydell Motors. Mr. Cordwin asked me to setcha up in his Jeep."

She'd thought of her new boss as "Dutch," and barely nodded before Billy Bob rambled on. Then she missed most of what he said because he grabbed her cart handle and took her by the elbow.

She snatched her arm away, but he didn't seem to notice.

"Right this way. Boy, Cordwin's gonna be one happy guy to get that Jeep today. Says he's never had a brand spankin' new set of wheels before. Ordered it special, he did. Nothin' but the best for Mr. Cordwin.''

Moira put on the brakes.

"Somethin' wrong, Miss Marshall?"

"How did you know I'd be here?"

"Mr. Cordwin told me to look for you on a plane in from Dallas."

"But I was due in yesterday."

"Yes, ma'am, I know." A gold tooth flashed when he smiled. "But you weren't here yesterday, so I came back last night, and again today. Mr. Cordwin wants his Jeep something bad, and I didn't want to disappoint him."

"I see."

"He could've come in himself, but it's a two-hour drive round trip, and I told him last week I'd get you all set up just fine." He reached for her arm again.

She scooted out of his reach. "I have to pick up my dog."

"Why, sure. Let's stow these bags first."

Moira wasn't sure whether she was miffed at not getting to do it all herself or grateful that someone walked her through it the first time around. With Billy Bob's help, she was soon sitting in a spotlessly clean, navy blue Jeep Wrangler in the parking lot. He'd stowed her luggage and saddle in the back seat. She had a map in her lap and handwritten directions taped lightly to the dash. Her half-drugged Australian shepherd—a hand-me-down from Chloe—was sprawled on the passenger seat, panting and shedding black and white fur all over it.

Unlike Chloe's vintage Jeep, on which Moira had received a couple of cursory lessons, this one had windows, which were unzipped and rolled over to the inside. Like Chloe's, it also had a stick shift. Nothing like making a fool of herself in front of a witness.

When she groaned, Billy Bob leaned close and studied her through narrowed eyes. "You *can* drive a stick, can't you?"

The real Chloe, whom Moira had known for ten years, had grown up in the wilds of Texas, hauling her horse from one rodeo to another. No one would believe Moira was Chloe if she couldn't carry this off.

Moira leaned away from him under the guise of patting the semiconscious dog. It was going to take a while to get used to people getting so close. "I was hoping I wouldn't have to."

"Hell, it ain't a real Jeep unless it's manual. Mr. Cordwin said you were from Texas. We just assumed you could drive a stick."

"It's been awhile," she said lamely. She remembered to affect a lingering accent, diminished by the years she and Chloe had been in Santa Barbara. "I, uh, broke my left ankle last year and had to have an automatic to get around."

The gold tooth flashed again. "Yeah, been there. Take my word for it, it's like ridin' a bike. By the time you get out on the highway, it'll all come back to you."

"I'm sure it will." She wished he'd walk away, but he waited. And he waited. She took a deep breath, pushed in the clutch and turned the key.

The engine roared to life. She put it in first gear, let out the clutch and promptly killed it. Billy Bob didn't say anything the first time. He leaned close again the second time, about to say something, when she successfully got it in gear and bolted away.

"Don't let him look," she prayed. Afraid she'd kill it again when she tried for second, she stayed in first as long as she could. "Make him go inside."

Second gear, like a second lie, was easier than first. She made it onto the highway, shifted again and headed for Dutch Cordwin's dude ranch.

Minutes flew by, like the breeze through the Jeep. Wisps of hair got loose from her cap and teased her cheek. She didn't care. She used to think a day in the condo without her maid and secretary underfoot was a day alone. Now as the miles added up on the new odometer, as she left traffic lights and telephones behind, as she traveled miles up into the mountains where ranches grew larger and farther apart, she learned what alone really was.

No secretary, no cook, no maid, no bodyguard. Just a dog who used to be Chloe's, who'd bite Moira's hand off if she gave it half a chance, and didn't look quite right as the tranquilizer wore off.

"Poor thing," Moira crooned. For the second time in the three years she'd known the dog, she reached out to pet it and didn't get growled at. Moira laughed. "Still drugged, huh?"

Friday panted. She coughed. At least Moira thought it was a cough until the dog's sides heaved and she brought up whatever had been in her stomach.

Moira looked at the mess on the seat and floor of Dutch's previously pristine Jeep. "And who do you think's going to clean that up?"

There wasn't enough shoulder to pull over onto. Even if there had been, she hadn't a clue how to clean up vomit. With the windows down and the wind blowing through, there was no noticeable odor. Unable to do anything about it just then, she ignored it.

The deep green of the pine forests both soothed and invigorated her. The air cooled as the road wound upward. Cattle seemed to be the main inhabitants of the region, followed by horses.

Friday finally rose to her feet, unfortunately tracking the semidry mess around on the seat, hung her head out the window and stayed there. The wind picked up the map and whisked it out Moira's window before she could catch it. Still adhered to the dash, the handwritten directions fluttered in the breeze, making them difficult to read.

The piercing wail of a siren surprised her. A patrol car appeared in her rearview mirror.

"What the heck am I supposed to do now?"

Friday peered over her shoulder at Moira and growled, long and low.

"Well, you're back to normal, I see." She nibbled her lower lip. "I know! I'll do what my limo driver always did." She slowed and pulled as far to the right as possible so the cop could pass.

Lights flashing, the patrol car eased up behind her. The siren had stopped—did that mean she didn't have to? She gently pressed on the accelerator. At the speed limit, he was still behind her. She passed a side road and was surprised when he not only didn't turn off, but revved up the siren again.

She turned onto the next dirt road, hoping that wasn't the one he'd wanted, praying he wouldn't give her a ticket for getting in his way.

He pulled in behind her. The road wasn't wide enough for him to go around. At a total loss, Moira stopped and waited for him to tell her what to do.

In her side mirror, she watched the uniformed patrolman get out of his car and approach. His boots crunched on gravel, and he didn't appear to be in any hurry now.

"Do you know why I pulled you over?" he asked.

"Pulled me—*me?*"

"Do you know the speed limit along here?"

"Uh…" Was this a test? Nothing like this had ever happened to her limo driver. "No."

"May I see your driver's license and registration, please?"

Moira suddenly felt light-headed. She wasn't sure if it was because, now that she'd stopped, she could smell the dog vomit, or because the only driver's license in her possession was Chloe's. She hadn't a clue about registration, what it was or where it was supposed to be.

"My license is in my purse. In…in the back. And I don't know where the registration is."

"Is this your vehicle?"

"No, it's my boss's. Dutch Cordwin."

He took a step back. Even though Moira couldn't see his eyes behind the reflective sunglasses, she would have sworn he cast an admiring eye over the vehicle. "Yeah, I see why he's been chomping at the bit ever since he ordered it. You delivering it?"

"Yes." *Too formal for a cowgirl.* "Uh, yeah. I'm the new ridin' instructor."

He nodded, kicked the front tire with the toe of his boot and appeared to size her up through his mirrored lenses. "Driver's license?"

She had to edge toward the dog in order to reach between the seats. Friday displayed her normal temperament—a low, rumbling growl. The cop leaned closer.

"My God, what *is* that smell?"

Moira had to admit, without the breeze blowing through, it was kind of overpowering. But she had bigger problems. Would he find the driver's license in order? She and Chloe looked so much alike, but the photograph on the license looked like a wanted poster.

"Got it."

Carlson, according to the name tag pinned on his shirt, took the license from her, glanced at it, scrutinized her, then started writing.

"What's the matter?" she asked.

"You were fifteen miles over the speed limit, Miss Marshall."

He'd bought it!

"Oh, uh, sorry."

He wrinkled his nose. "I almost hate to write you this ticket."

"You don't have to. Do you?"

"'Fraid I do. Want some advice?"

Do I have a choice? "What?"

"Dutch doesn't like nothing but the best. I wouldn't want to be in your boots when he sees what your dog's done." He held his little clip board out to her and pointed to the bottom. "Sign here. If I were you, I'd clean it out before he gets a whiff of it."

"For heaven's sake, it's just a car."

"Maybe to you, Miss Marshall. Maybe to you."

DUTCH CORDWIN had waited thirty-three years to earn respect, to make up for being born on the wrong side of the tracks. Every day he tried to drum it into his little girls that lying was wrong, that no good ever came of it when, in fact, he was standing on his very own ranch, which he'd earned through one whopper of a lie.

His momma probably had rolled over in her grave.

He could only console her that he was now able to give his big sister a job, he'd gotten custody of his twins and he provided honest employment for dozens of young men and women. And people *listened* to him, hung on his every word, asked his advice.

He shook his head in amazement at how the world could change in such a short time. He was dressed like any other honest-to-Pete cowboy in Colorado, but now when he walked into the bank, they shook his hand. When he rode across his ranch, his were the orders everyone followed. And when he'd strolled onto the car lot four weeks ago, the owner had brushed the salesmen aside and dealt with him man-to-man.

He'd ordered a navy Jeep that day, with tan soft top and upholstery. A rugged vehicle he could use for ranch work and hose out when it got dirty. The very same one he waited for now. And not very patiently, he had to admit, as he burst through the door of the dude ranch office and tossed his Resistol onto the file cabinet.

"Where the hell is my Jeep?"

A family of four, standing in front of the trail ride sign-up sheet, scuttled out of his way and out the door.

His older sister, MaryAnne, didn't even glance up from the ledger spread open on the desk in front of her. "Way to go, Dutch. Scare the guests silly."

Grinning sheepishly, he leaned out the door. "Sorry, folks."

When he straightened up and began pacing, MaryAnne asked, "Did that work?"

"Charmed the socks right off 'em." His boot heels thunked on the wood floor as he paced...door to window...window to door. Back again. "So where the hell's my Jeep?"

"Billy Bob called. It's on the way."

"It was supposed to be here yesterday."

Her sigh was inordinately loud. She looked up at him. "As long as you're in a snit, go fire that wrangler and let me work in peace."

"Tim? I can't fire him."

"Somebody has to."

"Not me."

"Dutch, he's not working out." She snorted. "Heck, what am I saying. He's barely working at all. He has to go."

"You'll have to do it."

MaryAnne surged to her feet and planted herself right in Dutch's path. "You know what your problem is?"

He held his ground, hooked his thumbs in his front jeans pockets and pointedly raised an eyebrow in her direction. "I hire people with no experience because I feel sorry for them?"

She poked him in the chest with her finger for emphasis. "Yeah, but I *learned* my job. He's worthless."

"He'll come around."

"Honestly, Dutch, you're just too bighearted."

"If my Jeep's not here in the next thirty seconds, you won't think so."

She threw her arms up. "I give up! You're like a bear with a thorn in its paw. Get outta here."

"I'm not—"

"You are!"

Dutch spun on his heel, stomped across the floor, grabbed his dark brown hat and wedged it on his head.

MaryAnne laughed. "When they hired you for that movie, did you tell them you weren't really acting? That deep down you're really the overly dramatic, hard-core cowboy they thought you were pretending to be?"

He graced her with his best scowl and as near as he could get to a John Wayne imitation. "If that's true, little lady, then your life's in danger."

She laughed even harder. "Get outta here."

"Laugh all you want now. As soon as the movie opens, the phone lines'll be jammed with people wanting reservations."

"Uh-huh."

He ignored her skepticism.

"How long ago did Billy Bob call?"

"One hour, fifteen minutes."

"It's only an hour's drive," he groused.

She pasted on a sugary smile. "Then it should be here any minute."

As soon as he was out of her sight, he rubbed the spot on his chest where she'd poked him. Maybe she was right; maybe he was a bit testy today. But he'd never bought a new Jeep before. He'd never bought a new *anything* before. For once he had money that didn't have to be split between his next two meals.

He dodged everyone at the barn, wranglers included, especially Tim—which wasn't too difficult because he was doing his best to dodge Dutch. Tim really needed to look for work elsewhere.

Quickly saddled up, Dutch headed cross-country on his big bay gelding, keeping the road in sight so he could intercept the Jeep when it arrived. *If* it arrived.

He didn't know Chloe Marshall from Eve. What if she decided a new Jeep was far and away better than working the summer in a hot, dusty corral? After all, instructing dudes in the simplest points of horsemanship was a bit beneath her, but she'd applied for the job and seemed pleased to get it, according to MaryAnne. On top of that, she'd been hired to teach his daughters everything budding little horsewomen needed to know. Three months wouldn't pay as much as a Jeep was worth. She could be halfway to Wyoming with it by now. Or headed back to Texas.

A dust cloud along the road caught his eye. He pulled up the gelding, waited and watched. It drew closer, headed for the ranch. His Jeep was on the way! With a whoop, he loped straight for the road, vaulted off his horse and hurdled the ditch.

He stood in the center of the dusty road and watched his brand-new Jeep—his toy, according to MaryAnne—slow to a crawl and stop twenty feet away.

A ball-capped head leaned out the window. "Get out of the way!"

He figured he probably looked a sight, a big, rough cowboy standing in the middle of the road grinning from ear to ear, but it was such a dang beautiful thing. The Jeep, not the woman. It didn't matter that he didn't get to put the first few miles on the odometer. It was still brand-new.

The woman wasn't bad, either.

So this is Chloe Marshall. When she turned her head, he caught a glimpse of a blond ponytail swinging out the back of her cap. It went with her face. Young and perky, full of life.

He strode forward for a better look, only to hear the gears grind as she put it in reverse and backed away. "Hey, wait!"

"Back off," she called out the window. The rear tire rolled perilously close to the edge of the road.

He stopped and threw his hands up, wondering whether he'd have to tow it out of the ditch before he got to drive it. "That's *my* Jeep."

"*Your* Jeep?" Her forehead puckered as she braked and studied him closer. "Who are you?"

"You're on the Cordwin Ranch, for God's sake. Who the hell do you think—"

She resumed her grinding retreat.

"No, no, wait. Don't back up any more. I'm Dutch Cordwin."

He must have been convincing, because she stopped, said, "Oh," and ground the gears into forward. It died. She tried again.

He clapped his hands over his ears. Better than wrapping them around her neck, which is what he wanted to do each time he heard metal mismesh with metal. "Stop! Please stop."

"Almost got it," she said, and the engine roared to life once again.

When it died, he rushed forward before she could do any more damage, yanked open the driver's door and ground out an uncivil, "Get out."

She shied toward the console. "What?"

"I'm driving from here."

She glanced at her dog. "But you can't—"

"The hell I can't." He wrapped his hand around her arm and tried unsuccessfully to ignore the fact that her face was a mirror of shock as he tugged her out. Like his sister, she was a good deal smaller than he. Unlike his sister, he noticed Chloe felt...like a woman. In spite of the Jeep sitting there, door open and begging him to slide behind the wheel for the first time, his hand lingered on her arm.

He told himself it was just to make sure she got her feet under her, but that was another whopper of a lie. His hesitation had little to do with that and everything to do with wondering why the heck he hadn't let go of her yet. Like any other cowgirl within a hundred miles, she wore scruffy boots, blue jeans and a button-up cotton shirt.

Unlike most others, he found her...distracting.

She jerked free of his grasp, looked indignant enough to chastise him for daring to lay a hand on her. "How dare you!"

She'd broken the spell, thankfully allowing him to come to his senses. He turned and stroked the navy paint with a lover's touch, moving the dust around. The finish was unscratched. There were no dents. He really needed to calm down. She was a cowgirl from Texas; of course she knew how to drive. The new clutch was probably just too stiff for her petite—and very shapely—frame.

When the Jeep started to roll backward, Dutch jumped in, brought it to a standstill and cranked the parking brake. He noticed a piece of paper on the floor that looked like...no, it couldn't be. He reached down and picked it up.

"A speeding ticket!"

She edged away, toward the center of the road.

·"You've been speeding in my new Jeep?" he demanded. "You're supposed to break it in gently." He ran his hands lovingly over the steering wheel, the dash, the console.

The dog growled.

"Shut up."

It showed its teeth.

He was about to tell it to take a flying leap out the window—and he'd be glad to help—when he got a whiff of something that didn't belong in any new vehicle. "What's that?" He inhaled deeply and gagged.

He bolted out of the Jeep and gasped in fresh air.

"We, uh, had a little accident," Chloe said.

He stalked toward her. "What in tarnation is that smell?"

She took three steps backward, then stood her ground. "I know she doesn't get car sick, so I guess it was air sickness, or the tranquilizer or something."

Words eluded him. He felt his mouth open and close, but nothing came out.

She closed the gap between them and peered up at him. "Are you okay?"

"Huh?"

"Your eyes look kind of glazed over." She waved her hand in front of his face. "It's not that bad."

He caught her wrist in his hand, the speeding ticket layered between his palm and her skin. Is this the woman he wanted to teach his daughters *any*thing?

No way.

"You're fired."

Her mouth dropped open. She twisted her wrist, but she only got loose when he remembered to release her. "You can't fire me."

"I just did."

"But—"

"But first, you drive my *brand-new*—" he put a lot of emphasis on the last two words "—Jeep up the hill to the laundry. I want you to hose it out real good before you hitch a ride back to the airport."

He collected his gelding and parked himself in the center of the road behind the Jeep, just in case she decided to try to drive away with it.

"Well, go on. Get behind the wheel," he roared.

He heard her own dog growl at her when she put one foot up into the Jeep. She turned her back to it and eased in.

"And don't grind the gears anymore!"

She did.

HER LEFT ARM still tingled from when Dutch had pulled her out of the Jeep. Her right wrist burned from his strong grasp. The dog could have bitten her when she reached for the stick shift, and Moira doubted she would have noticed. Her encounter with the tall, broad-chested cowboy left her with a myriad of emotions—most of which were very confusing.

Billy Bob's pumping handshake hadn't left her feeling as if…she'd been branded. As if her brain had been short-circuited. He and Dutch both lived in Colorado and both wore cowboy hats and boots, so her response wasn't to anything geographical or sartorial.

No, it was something more. Chloe would call it "man-woman stuff." Hormones. Chemistry. Until now, Moira had never really understood what all that meant. Having just gotten close enough to stare into his eyes, though—which were the shade of sinfully rich fudge—she got the picture.

Why now? When he'd fired her.

And could he do that? She'd never had a boss before, so she wasn't sure. What would Chloe do?

Well, Chloe could always go back to Texas and find someone she used to rodeo with, or someone she'd grown up with, but any of those people would recognize Moira as an impostor.

Hitchhiking wasn't safe, she knew that. She might have been a princess, but she hadn't been kept in a locked room. Besides, who would pick her up with Chloe's dog snarling at them? No, she'd have to find another way back to the airport.

She slammed her palm on the steering wheel. What was she thinking? She wasn't a wealthy princess anymore. She wasn't about to sell her pearl necklace—the only memento of her mother that Moira had kept, safely hidden away. She had no money for an airline ticket to who-knew-where. She'd have to get to the nearest town, find a cheap place to stay and apply for a job. To do that, she'd need transportation.

She'd need the Jeep a little longer. She wrinkled her nose; it really had to be cleaned out first. Now where was that laundry Dutch mentioned? And how did a hose work?

DUTCH STORMED into the office, letting the door slam behind him hard enough to rattle the glass. "MaryAnne, get on the phone."

His blond-haired, blue-eyed daughters jumped at his bark. With one long braid each, the eight-year-olds were as identical in pink-flowered shirts and blue jeans as two peas in a pod. They framed MaryAnne in her chair like bookends.

With them in the office, he had to watch his language. "Find us a new riding instructor."

"What happened to Chloe?"

"I fired her."

"Dad-dy," Katie and Nicole whined in unison.

Eyes twinkling, MaryAnne's mouth dropped open. "*You* fired her?"

"She ruined my Jeep."

MaryAnne surged to her feet and headed for the door. "She wrecked it? Is she hurt? Should I call a doctor?"

Dutch clamped his mouth shut. Okay, so maybe he was being a little overly dramatic. He took a deep breath, flung his hat onto the file cabinet and raked his fingers through his dark hair. "No, she didn't wreck it. She's fine. She just messed it up inside."

He didn't like the way his "big" sister studied him.

"And *you* fired her?"

He nodded, afraid to say more for fear she'd laugh at him.

"But, Daddy, you promised," the twins both whined, saving him from his sister's scrutiny.

"MaryAnne'll find someone else." He flung his arms open wide and grinned. "How're my girls?"

For the first time in the twelve months he'd had them, they didn't budge. Their expressions said it all. He'd promised them a summer of personalized riding instruction. English for Nicole, who wanted to learn dressage and jumping. Western for Katie, who had her sights set on rodeoing. Chloe Marshall's résumé listed the former, but the grapevine mentioned an impressive rodeo history for her, too.

"She was the best all-around candidate, Dutch."

"You said never to break a promise," Katie reminded him.

At least he thought it was Katie. "Don't worry, honey. We'll find someone else."

"Never break a promise," Nicole echoed. "You said it's just as important as telling the truth—"

"—and only trouble comes from not telling the truth—"

"—like that spider story."

All three females glared at him, though Mary-Anne's carried a hint of amusement behind it. His daughters were definitely not amused. A person could take one look at them and think he'd just shot their favorite horses.

In the future, he'd have to watch what promises he made. He was only guilty of wanting to give them everything now that he had the means. He'd be sure MaryAnne found someone else quickly.

"Spider story?" he asked weakly.

"Tangled web stuff," MaryAnne explained.

"Ah." From experience, he understood that well enough. "Find someone else. Pronto."

Both girls stamped their feet, crossed their arms over their little chests and stuck out a matching set of lower lips.

"Sure," MaryAnne agreed too easily. "But now that you've got experience, I'll get on the phone and find you a new riding instructor as soon as you go fire—" she glanced at the puckered-eyed twins "—that wrangler we talked about."

"Why? He didn't ruin my Jeep."

She glanced out the window. "Forget your Jeep."

"Forget my—"

"She just drove away with it."

He caught a glimpse of rear bumper pulling around the curve, taillights flashing red as Chloe slowed for a guest. Without a backward glance, he fled the office, jumped off the porch and beat any Pony Express record for mounting a horse. He took care going downhill and where the ground was rough, but otherwise galloped straight cross-country. Chloe had to follow every twist and turn of the road, negotiate strolling guests and children, and fumble with the gears. He'd be lucky if it had any left by the time he caught up with her.

And catch up he did, though when his big bay leapt the gully and landed in the road, Chloe overcompensated and swerved too far to the right. The Jeep bounced across the ditch, mowed down a score of saplings and came to rest on an angle with the passenger side higher than the driver's. The dog was nowhere in sight.

The grapevine had also said Chloe Marshall was a woman who'd held her own growing up with a half dozen wild foster brothers and could do a handstand on a galloping horse. It hadn't said she could drive worth a darn. He'd just assumed it.

Apparently he'd been wrong.

He reached for the door, but she was leaning on it. If he wrenched it open, she'd tumble out onto the ground. He might be mad at her, but he wasn't hankerin' to see her hurt any.

"You all right?" he asked.

She sputtered and waved away the dust billowing around her. The dog, sopping wet, scrambled from the floor onto the far seat. Dutch shook his head. It figured if she was going to let the dog throw up on his upholstery that she'd let it ride sopping wet on it, too.

"Yes, I believe I'm all right."

She sounded mighty prissy for a cowgirl.

"Hold on to the wheel. I'm going to open the door and help you out."

He pulled on the handle. As the door fell open, he opened his arms to catch her if need be. Instead, a flash flood of ice-cold water drenched him from the thighs down, turning his jeans a deeper shade of blue. Speechless, he watched it run off and turn the dirt at his feet into a steadily darkening ring of mud.

It gave him time to figuratively stand back and take a closer look at what had just happened.

He hadn't reached in the window and wrung her neck. He hadn't run to the front and checked out the damage. He hadn't yanked open the door and let her tumble into the dirt. Why was that?

He refused to think about the implications just then.

"Anybody ever tell you Jeeps have drain plugs?" he asked instead.

"Oh."

"Yeah. Oh." He ducked his head, reached in and scooped her into his arms. As he drew her up close and straightened his back, she fit nicely against his chest. Warm and soft, with the fragrance of lilacs tumbling off her hair now that the ball cap was history. Her legs draped nicely over his arm, with her jeans rolled halfway up to her knees and her feet bare.

Now what the heck do I do with her?

He picked his way back to the flat of the road, his stride hampered by the stiffness of wet denim.

I promised Katie and Nicole.

Slowly he set her on her feet, holding her against him longer than necessary. Long enough to find out that the top of her head didn't quite reach his chin, and her eyes were hazel. If the sudden gold sparks in them hadn't telegraphed her intentions, he probably would've been decked by the punch she threw at his jaw. As it was, he had plenty of time to block, catching her fist in his hand with a resounding *smack* of soft skin pillowed against calluses.

Her eyes rounded with surprise.

He knew he should fire her again. Not that he'd rehired her yet, but he was going to and he knew it. His promise to Katie and Nicole demanded it.

Heck, who was he kidding? They were only eight years old. His body demanded it. It was thirty-three and knew a worthy challenge.

His grin was meant to reassure her. "It's not nice to try and punch your boss."

"You're not my boss. You fired me."

He nearly pulled her knuckles to his lips, but common sense overrode that desire. "Yeah, well, I was under a lot of stress at the moment."

She had the good grace to nibble her lip. "I know. I'm sorry about your Jeep. It hosed out nicely, though."

He waggled one drenched leg for effect. "Yeah, so I see."

She turned her head—giving him a lovely profile of long eyelashes, high cheekbones and a perfect nose—and studied the crooked Jeep. "I'm afraid it's probably a little more serious now."

He sighed. "Never mind. I was just all worked up because..." He didn't know what to say.

"Yeah, I heard. It was new. Billy Bob said it was your first time."

He felt his lips twitch. He dropped her hand and rubbed his across his mouth, trying to stifle—or at least hide—the grin that threatened to spread. A sum-

mer with this gal was bound to be instructive for
everyone.

"Forget I fired you, okay?"

Her smile radiated all the way through her, spar-
kling in her eyes, perking up her posture. He'd swear
it even brought life back to her ponytail.

"No more goof-ups, though. No trouble, or else."
Before he was tempted to soften the warning, he
stalked back across the ditch, retrieved her boots and
tossed them into the dust, then slid behind the steering
wheel. The dog, as feisty as her owner, greeted him
with a low, rumbling growl. "And that goes double
for your dog."

MOIRA SAT ON DUTCH'S HORSE and watched his wide
shoulders bunch and dip as he shifted gears and wres-
tled with the steering wheel. His face was a study of
determination. His lips moved occasionally, probably
with curses, until he finally maneuvered the Jeep
across the ditch and onto the road.

She knew she should have told him that she didn't
want any special treatment. She'd had enough of that
to last her a lifetime—she wouldn't have told him that
part—but she was afraid she could barely say anything coherent at all. Just as well, because special
treatment this time meant she got to keep her job.

Other than a few well-screened escorts in college,
she'd never been so close to a man, never been
scooped up and carried next to one's hard chest, never
known a man like Dutch existed outside the movies.
Mel, Alec, Antonio—she'd thought no one could live
up to their screen personae.

She was wrong. If her racing heart and sweaty
palms were any indication, if the feeling in her stom-

ach was the butterflies she'd heard other women talk about, she knew she'd just encountered a real live hunk.

Or maybe it was just because, unlike Billy Bob, Dutch was a real down-to-earth cowboy. The jeans, the horse, the ranch, the whole bit. He looked as rugged as the mountain she'd driven up and didn't appear to have a spare ounce of fat on him, though she certainly wouldn't call him lean. Words like "range-hewn" and "steel-corded" came to mind, and she had to wonder when they'd slipped into her vocabulary. Undoubtedly too many years of being friends with Chloe.

If it was just a cowboy thing, maybe there were wranglers on this dude ranch who'd make her blood boil, too.

She had a whole summer to find out.

Chapter Two

At the top of the hill, around a curve, Moira got a much better look at the main body of the dude ranch from the back of Dutch's horse than she had the first time she'd driven through, when she'd been looking for the laundry and wondering how to work a hose. She'd figured out how to operate one soon enough, when she should have been more concerned about the growing amount of water accumulating on the floor of the Jeep.

There was just so much for a princess to learn about being "average."

The only part she'd found similar to being royal, so far, was that sticking up for herself worked just as well as giving orders. As Princess Moira, she would have summoned someone to drive her back to the airport. As Chloe, she'd asserted her right to "borrow" Dutch's Jeep—and now she had her job back. Amazing! If the rest of the summer went this easily, she had nothing to worry about.

The road ended in a replica of a town square. Several buildings, which looked as authentic as anything she'd seen in a Western movie, bore old-fashioned signs which read Saloon—Home Cookin', Sheriff,

General Store, Barber Shop—where she'd found the laundry, and Ma's Boarding House. Dutch's Jeep sat in front of the latter. A weathered Conestoga wagon, with several small children climbing on it, rested near the store. Hitching posts and water troughs fronted the boardwalks, as if waiting for trail hands to ride in and tie up.

Off to the left of the square, partially hidden in the pines along a narrow, winding track, were A-frame cabins for the guests.

Since she'd arrived, Moira had seen a dozen women strolling to the barn, watching the children, looking relaxed and happy on their vacation. They all wore jeans. Most had straw cowboy hats. Some wore Western shirts.

One woman stood out. As soon as she stepped out of the sheriff's office, family resemblance alone indicated this had to be Dutch's older sister, MaryAnne, who'd hired Moira sight unseen. The same dark hair and dark eyes looked as feminine on her as they did all male on him.

"Hi. I'm MaryAnne," she confirmed with a welcoming smile.

"Hi, I'm Moi...mighty pleased to meet you." *Well, that sounded pretty stupid, Moira.* She quickly dismounted, rounded the gelding's head and stuck out her hand. "I'm Chloe."

MaryAnne's handshake was as warm as her smile. "Not half as glad as I am to see that my brother left you and the dog in one piece." She gestured toward Ma's Boarding House. "That's the girls' dorm. Go on in, find yourself a bunk and unpack. Here, leave the horse with me." She took the reins. "Then meet me in the General Store. We'll have some ice cream and go over your schedule.''

''Sounds great.'' Hot and tired from her trip, that was an understatement.

As Moira unloaded her belongings, she experienced a pang of longing for her baggage master. He would have carried the heavy suitcases into her room. Her personal maid would have handled the unpacking. Then there'd be nothing to do but race over to the General Store for that ice cream. Double Chocolate Cherry Chip Brownie would be nice. Two scoops.

But she had no baggage master, no personal maid. She wanted to be anonymous, to be treated like anyone else, to manage for herself the same as everyone else.

Friday, no worse for her trip up the hill with Dutch, sat patiently on the passenger seat. Moira could only guess that the dog somehow felt closer to Chloe in there. It was certain she hadn't adjusted to Moira yet.

Saddle over her arm, she wandered into Ma's Boarding House.

So this is what a dormitory looks like. A long hallway ran straight back, doors on both sides stood ajar. The first bedroom on the left had two bare bunks and two small, four-drawer dressers. Other rooms, as she walked down the hall, had one or both bunks made up, linens crumpled, socks hanging out of drawers.

The bathroom was at the far end of the building, which explained why the first bedroom was still vacant. While she didn't expect to find a marble sink and gold faucets, the five porcelain sinks bolted in a row along the left wall were a bit of a shock, highlighted as they were by the blinking fluorescent fixture overhead. Toilet stalls were to the right.

A doorway on the far wall led to four shower stalls. Each had a flimsy plastic curtain, a tiny shelf for soap or shampoo, and a drain in the center of its concrete floor. The only positive thing she could say for the whole bathroom was that it appeared reasonably clean. Other than that, she'd seen enough.

Rather than move in with someone who might not want a roommate—it appeared she'd get to know everyone well enough in the bathroom—she took the first bedroom. She dropped her saddle on the bunk closer to the door and returned outside to find Friday lying across the seat, panting hard.

"Unless there's still water on the floor, you're going to have to come out of there for a drink," Moira told her. A cursory exam showed that Dutch had opened the drain plugs. "Come on." It was no surprise that the dog didn't budge. "Out. Now."

"Trouble?"

The deep baritone startled Moira, not because she didn't know who it was, but because she hadn't heard Dutch approach. When she turned, she found quite a sight—the tall, dark cowboy flanked by the cutest pair of little blond twins, identical right down to their dusty jeans and chocolate-stained shirts.

"Uh, no. No trouble."

Friday's rumble made a liar out of her.

"Your dog doesn't appear too happy to be here."

"She, uh, didn't like the plane ride, I guess."

He wore his dark hat low, shading his eyes, making her want to lift the brim for a closer look. The casual way he splayed his hands on his hips made his chest broader, his shoulders wider.

Moira was in a sudden rush to meet some of the wranglers and see if they had the same effect on her.

She was in big trouble either way; nothing in her sheltered life had prepared her for a man like Dutch. If there were more of them running around, she'd be like a starving woman in an ice cream factory.

"She can't stay if she's not friendly," he warned.

She hauled her mind back to the issue at hand, before she and the dog found themselves standing outside the front gate. After all, she'd promised Chloe she'd take care of the dog, so if Friday was kicked off the ranch, Moira had to go, too.

"Give her a day for the tranquilizer to wear off." *Give me a day to get her into my room and shut the door.* "She'll adjust."

"Well, I need to move my Jeep, so she'll have to adjust somewhere else. We keep this area clear of vehicles so it's safe for all the kids."

Moira turned to Friday and gave her the sweeping hand signal she'd seen Chloe use so many times to send the dog on its way. "Go play."

Nothing happened, not that she'd expected it to, but she'd hoped for the best. One look over her shoulder at Dutch, and she knew she and her dog were being put to the test. He'd already warned her that he didn't want any more trouble. There was only one thing left to do.

She strode over to the open door, quickly and with purpose, hoping to shock Friday into muteness. She grabbed her by the collar and dragged her out of the Jeep, raising a cloud of dust where she landed on her belly. If looks could kill, the one Friday graced Moira with would have turned her into ashes on the spot.

Moira mentally counted all her fingers to be sure she still had them. She glanced at Dutch to see whether he was going to erupt.

Friday belly-crawled—Moira thought the dog had missed her chance at Hollywood—halfway to Dutch and the girls.

"Is she—" one twin began.

"—sick?" the other finished.

"No, she's just a little drugged." *Can I say "drugged" to little children?*

Friday yipped at the girls, flipped over onto her back, whined and let her tongue loll out the side of her mouth. Her stubby tail wagged up a dust bath.

The twins were on their knees before Moira could even think about warning them off, which was pretty fast considering she still carried the scars from a long-ago dog attack. They rubbed her belly, petted her face and raised even more dust. She squirmed and scratched her back. And appeared to be smiling.

Probably laughing at me. "You girls must be pretty special. She doesn't take to everyone." Which was the understatement of the year.

"She's nicer—"

"—than the barn dogs."

Dutch eased his hat back a notch as, pride written all over his face, he watched his daughters. Moira regretted her father had never looked at her like that. If he had, just one time in her whole life, she'd still be a king's daughter.

"This is Katie," Dutch introduced the one nearer him, "and that's Nicole."

Both girls giggled. "Dad-dy!"

He rubbed his hand over the back of his neck and shook his head. The grin he flashed at Moira was slightly sheepish, amused and perplexed at the same time. It made her stomach feel all fluttery inside and her heart jump-started right into heavy-duty pitter-patter. If every cowboy on the ranch grinned like that, she'd never make it through the summer.

"Wrong again, I guess. I swear, if they don't stop dressing alike, I'm gonna have to brand them."

Katie and Nicole giggled even more, Katie so hard that she fell over onto her back in the dust. Moira barely heard them, though. She was too busy trying to blame her symptoms on the long trip.

"You go ahead and unpack," Dutch said. "Your first lesson's in the corral in thirty minutes."

No ice cream? "But, MaryAnne said—"

"I told her you'd be available later. Come on, girls." Dutch held out a hand to each of them, which they readily grabbed. As they walked away, he tossed over his shoulder, "Don't be late."

Be late to see him again? He had to be joking.

"WE LIKE HER—"

"—so when do we get our lesson?"

Dutch ushered Katie and Nicole into the office. "Later. You girls stay with MaryAnne until four o'clock. Then you can come on down to the corral for your lesson. Okay?"

"Okay—"

"—Daddy."

MaryAnne, who'd been sitting at her desk, chewing the eraser on her pencil until Dutch got his hugs and kisses from the girls, jumped up as he headed for the door. "Wait a minute."

"I've got to get down to the corral."

"Unless you're in a hurry to fire someone," she said pointedly, "we've got another problem."

He gave in with a sigh. For someone who'd had no experience running an office before he gave her the job, she'd learned entirely too well. Unlike most intelligent people, she wasn't intimidated by him in the least.

"We just had a man drive in and sign up as a guest."

"Way up here?" They were a bit off the beaten path for spur-of-the-moment guests.

"Mmm, that's what I thought. And he asked about riding lessons."

Dutch resisted the urge to laugh outright. "Well, that is strange. A man comes to a dude ranch and wants to learn how to ride."

"Shut up and listen to me. This is really strange, Dutch. He's no dude. He carried himself like a well-worn range hand. Why, at first I thought he was here to apply for a wrangler job."

"Any family with him?" Not that it mattered a whole hell of a lot. They were in business to take guests, after all.

"Nope, just him. He said he'd seen the new riding instructor and didn't want to miss the afternoon lesson, so you'll probably find him there."

Dutch shrugged. "So Chloe has an admirer already. So what?" His indifference didn't ring true, even to him, but there was no way he was going to spend time sorting through his reaction to Chloe in front of his sister.

As it was, she frowned at him. "She just got here."

"And your point is?"

"Maybe he followed her. Maybe she's got a stalker."

"Dammit, MaryAnne, you lived in the city too long. What do you want me to do? Interrogate the guy under a bare lightbulb?"

"Just look into it. Talk to him and see what you think."

He nodded. "Okay. No problem."

"And be careful. He's bigger than you."

DUTCH SAT TALL and straight on his bay gelding in the center of the corral, in front of a line of mounted guests. In a matter of minutes, he'd quickly weeded out the ones who didn't need a beginner course and sent them out for a trail ride with Wade, a college student wrangling for the summer.

Dutch was patiently explaining the basic commands to the ten who remained. "To stop, pull back gently on the reins and say 'whoa.'" He noticed none of the men were paying any attention. They all seemed to be focused on a spot behind him.

Glancing over his shoulder, he saw why. Chloe, in a red tank top, curve-hugging tan jodhpurs, and brown paddock boots, was a sight for any man's eyes. Her ponytail was pulled through the back of her Dodgers cap again and seemed to be in perpetual motion as she jogged up to the rail. That wasn't all that bounced, but it was all he allowed himself to think about, otherwise he'd ride over there, pull her up behind him and lope off to a secluded spot.

"Sorry I'm late," she said.

The shy smile she flashed everyone earned her instant forgiveness, if the guests' answering smiles were any indication. Men and women both.

"Folks, this is Chloe. As soon as she gets on that little pinto there—" he pointed out the horse he wanted her to ride "—right, that's the one. Mount up and come on in here." He turned back to the guests.

"She's going to teach you how to go, how to stop, how to turn right and left."

He'd already given them his spiel on the importance of doing everything quietly around the horses, how they'd all been carefully selected by him and were very reliable. Good thing, too, because as soon as Chloe rode up beside him, he inhaled the scent of fresh lilacs and forgot everything else.

"Did you get that?" he asked for her ears only.

"Stop, go, right, left." She smiled. "Yeah, I got it."

Another good thing, because as soon as her lips parted in a smile prettier than a mountain sunrise, he forgot his name, too.

"You could've hired someone a whole lot cheaper than me to teach that."

It was his turn to grin. "Yeah, well, wait'll you mount up the twins."

On that note, he rode out of the corral. He felt her eyes on his back as he left, sizing him up, making his skin tingle. But when he turned to meet her gaze, her attention was firmly riveted on the dudes.

She smiled at them, she instructed them in simple terms without talking down to them, she gently coaxed them into sitting up straight and moving their horses around her in a circle at a walk. He found no fault with her teaching method.

He also knew his two darling daughters could be a whole lot more active on horseback than ten of the greenest dudes. If she could handle them, he could reap the benefits—or purgatory—of standing by and watching Chloe, without interruption, for a whole hour.

MOIRA ENJOYED THE GUESTS' lesson immensely, even though, toward the end of it, her mind wandered a bit to the three college-age wranglers standing by. They were there, she knew, to help with the horses if need be, and to help the guests dismount when they were through. Dutch had watched for a while, then disappeared into the barn.

She wanted to end the lesson and talk to those wranglers. She wanted to see if their faces were carved of hard angles that softened when they smiled—as Dutch's did. She wondered if one of them laughed at something she said, would the sound make her heart go pitter-patter?

When the lesson was over, as she and the wranglers helped the guests dismount and tie their horses, two little voices piped up. Katie and Nicole had arrived.

"Hey, Chloe, we—"

"—brought you some lemonade."

While the old Moira would have smiled and said a polite "Thank you," the new one came up with, "That's mighty nice of you girls." She was quite proud of herself. Other than the one small slip she'd made in front of MaryAnne, she was pleased that she'd stayed in character quite nicely.

"We're ready—"

"—for our lesson now."

So much for time to hang out with a few of the guys. "Okay, which horses are yours?"

"They're in the barn. We'll be—"

"—right back with 'em."

The wrangler nearest Moira chuckled and said, "Cuter 'n a pair of speckled pups, ain't they?"

His chuckle didn't do a thing for her heart rate. For future reference, just in case, Moira filed away the information that speckled pups were cute. She was supposed to be from Texas; she was sure she was supposed to know phrases like that. "Yeah, they sure are."

Katie and Nicole returned, each leading a well-groomed horse in Western tack. Dutch followed, his long legs reined in to the shorter stride.

Moira held the corral gate open. "Okay, girls, lead them in and mount up."

"We can't get on by ourselves. They're—"

"—too tall."

"Do you girls always finish each other's sentences?"

"Uh-huh, 'cause we not only look alike—"

"—we think alike."

"I see." She turned to Dutch, who'd just slipped through the gate and headed for his daughters. "Well, I guess we need smaller horses for these girls so they can get on by themselves."

A little cloud of dust billowed up where he ground to a halt. Katie and Nicole glanced at each other, then scrambled into their saddles.

Dutch muttered, "Well, I'll be damned."

One of the girls gasped. The other said, "Daddy!"

"Okay," Moira said, "who's who?"

"I'm Katie," said the one on the buckskin gelding. "I want to ride in rodeos."

"I'm Nicole," said the one on the white gelding. "I want to learn dressage and jumping."

Something didn't look right to Moira. "Why don't you two take five minutes to warm up and show me what you know?"

Within thirty seconds, it was apparent what was wrong. The twin who'd said she wanted to rodeo was never going to make it riding with two hands on the reins like that. And the other, who'd said she wanted to learn dressage, neck-reined like a pro.

Reminded of how she and Chloe had traded places on more than one occasion, Moira grinned. She walked over to the rail where Dutch had parked himself. "Do they try to fool everyone?"

"Huh?"

"Unless I miss my guess, they've switched places."

His back went ramrod straight. When he opened his mouth, she knew he intended to bellow at them.

"Hush." She winked. "It's no big deal."

"The hell it's not."

"Relax, it's my lesson." She pushed away from the fence. "Okay, girls, come here." When they halted their horses in front of her, she said, "I've got a dressage saddle up in my room. Who'd like to use it?"

When the real Nicole nearly bounced out of her saddle with excitement, their masquerade was up.

"Nicole, you gave us away!"

"I don't care. A real dressage saddle? Really? You'd let me use it on Prince Charming?"

"Sure." Moira turned to Dutch. "Go get my saddle. It's up on my bed."

When the only muscle he moved was the one that twitched in his jaw, she realized she'd fallen back into princess-to-servant mode. She did the only thing she could think of: she smiled repentantly.

"Oops, sorry." She felt her cheeks heat, too, which was probably a nice effect because Dutch's ramrod-straight posture relaxed a little. "Please?"

He yelled for Tim, while she gave herself a mental slap upside the head as a reminder to be more careful.

"When can I learn to do tricks?"

Moira smiled up at Katie, glad for the diversion. "You mean like trading places with your sister?" Amused, she watched as they switched mounts without ever getting below the horses' shoulders.

"No, I mean like a reverse sender or a death drag."

"Your dad didn't mention you liked trick riding." From the open expression on his face, he didn't seem opposed.

Unfortunately trick riding was Chloe's specialty, not Moira's. But she suspected she'd been hired because someone *thought* she could do both.

"Well, sweetheart, let's see how you do with the basics first, okay?"

And give me time to figure out how the heck I'm going to teach you trick riding without your dad figuring out I'm not who he thinks I am.

AFTER THE LESSON, Dutch walked Katie and Nicole back up the hill to the town square. They babbled on and on about their lesson and Chloe.

"So, you liked her?" Dutch asked when he could get a word in edgewise.

"Yeah, Daddy."

"Then why'd you swap places?"

Instant silence. Katie's interest suddenly centered on a rock she found to kick up the hill in front of her. Nicole studied the sky. At least, he thought Katie had the rock and Nicole was the one looking up. He'd had them for twelve months and still hadn't a clue, wasn't sure whether twelve years would make a difference. They really were identical.

"We've talked about this before, you know. It's not nice to fool people." Still no answer. "You'll have to give up your dessert tonight."

"But you—"

"—fool people."

Did they know what he'd done? "How's that?" he asked innocently. He hadn't starred in a movie for no reason.

"In the movies, you're just—"

"—pretending."

He nodded. "That's true. But that's honest work. That's what acting is all about, and people know when they see it that it's not real. When you're not honest with people, it's the same as lying."

"We're sorry, Daddy. Do you—"

"—like her?"

He was taken aback by the quick change in direction and the ease with which they took their punishment. "Well, sure I do." *In more ways than one.*

"Good, so she can—"

"—stay?"

"Yes, she can stay."

Their little furrowed frowns disappeared.

"I liked her saddle, too. Can you buy me one in my size?"

He grinned, not at Nicole's question, but as he recalled Chloe's shy smile when she realized she'd just bossed the boss around. She'd backpedaled nicely. "I don't know if they make 'em in tadpole size."

"Dad-dy!"

"Okay, okay." He gently tugged the long, loose braid hanging down the center of her back. "I'll check."

"And I want riding britches like hers, too."

"They're sure different, aren't they?" Snug, curve-hugging wonders that made him want to burn her jeans.

"Yeah, Daddy. She told me they're all stretchy and comfy. Not like jeans."

When he could wrench his mind off Chloe's legs in tight tan jodhpurs, he saw the benefits of his two little munchkins not dressing alike. "I'll get right on it."

"When can I start doing tricks?" Katie asked.

"Basics first, remember?"

"But you said when she got here."

"Well, she's here now. And she's boss of your lessons."

Katie stuck out her lower lip.

"Well..." he relented. "Maybe she can show you a trick or two if you're a really good student."

He wouldn't mind seeing the legendary Chloe Marshall do some of her stunts. It would entertain the guests, too. Not like it would him, though. They'd be all agoggle at how anyone could ride a horse at high speeds in such untraditional positions. He, on the other hand, would be extremely glad to have the opportunity to stare at her body without looking like a lecher.

Chapter Three

The supper bell rang at six o'clock sharp, drawing Moira into the Saloon for the promised "Home Cookin'." Inside, it looked nothing like a saloon. It was a large, open, airy room, with golden wood from the sky-high ceiling down to the floors. A touch of color came from the Native American blanket hanging over the loft rail. Framed photographs of the surrounding San Juan Mountains ranged from spring green to winter wonderland white.

Dutch strode up beside Moira, one giggly twin tucked under each arm until they wiggled free and raced off to join MaryAnne. "We dine family style here," his deep voice rumbled quietly just above her ear. "The staff is expected to spread out, eat with the guests, mix and mingle."

She'd never "mingled" in her life.

With a dip of his head, he indicated a nearby table with two adults and three children. "Take that table over there this evenin'. Dave's got a real nice family."

A family. She'd always yearned to be a part of one. She'd seen them on TV. Dave's appeared pretty average. Father, mother, teenage boy, younger brother and sister. No hugging, no snarling.

"They said I can go to Mesa Verde with them later in the week," the older boy told his parents with a measure of excitement.

"What a wonderful opportunity," his mother replied. She looked up as Moira hovered behind one of two empty chairs. "You must be the new riding instructor."

Moira nodded. "Yeah."

"Don't be shy, dear. Have a seat."

She pulled out the chair, only to have a wrangler—Donny, she thought—grab her lightly by the arm as he rushed by. "Can't sit just yet. We have to get the food."

She followed him to a very long table, laden with platters and bowls of food, against the side wall. She wasn't too busy to notice that his grasp had felt nothing like Dutch's. Her arm didn't tingle or burn. Her heart didn't flip-flop.

Following Donny's example, she scooped up a plate of pork chops and a bowl of gravy and delivered them to her table, then went back for mashed potatoes and green beans. By the time she returned again, Dutch had settled himself in the empty chair beside hers.

"Have y'all met our new riding instructor?" As she took her seat, he laid his hand along the back of it for a gentle, unnecessary assist. "This is Chloe. Chloe, this is Dave, Nancy, Bob, Billy, and Bethanie."

"Nice to meet you," Nancy said. Dave nodded in agreement as he speared the first chop. The kids gave her a cursory glance and followed their father's example.

"Nice to meet y'all, too," Moira replied, quite pleased to discover that the Texas lingo she'd accumulated over the years would fit in well in Colorado, too.

As Dutch mounded a big scoop of potatoes onto his plate, he bumped elbows with her. "'Scuse me," he said.

Without his hat to shade his eyes, she could see a twinkle in there. She suspected he didn't regret their contact at all. Nor did she, though she doubted he'd ever understand what it meant to her. Even she was just beginning to realize how starved she was for normal, everyday touching.

"No problem." She yearned to bump him back when she reached for the green beans, but she wasn't brave enough. Not yet. She needed more practice being plain ol' average before she tried flirting.

"You don't sound much like you're from Texas."

Oh God. "Oh?"

"I expected more of a drawl."

"Oh. Well, I've lived in Santa Barbara for years."

As if that was expected, he didn't dwell on it. "So, Dave, how'd the trail ride go this morning?"

When his knee brushed against hers, then came to rest there, the whole room and everyone in it faded into nothing more than a low hum in her ear.

Okay, so she'd talked to one wrangler and it hadn't made her heart flutter. And she'd been touched by Donny and had no trouble hearing eighty guests around her.

It was Dutch, pure and simple, that made her blood simmer. What was she to do now? She had no experience with this. She'd expected... Well, she didn't know what she'd expected, but certainly not a cowboy whose touch made her forget to breathe. At this rate, she'd be comatose by midnight.

"Chloe?" Nancy asked.

Moira focused on the curious faces around the table and suspected she'd missed a question. "Sorry." She covered with a laugh. "I guess I've had a long day. Did you ask me something?"

"Yes, dear. I'm curious what you do the rest of the year. You know, when you're not working on a dude ranch."

What the heck was on my résumé? "I go to college in Santa Barbara."

Nancy visibly perked up. "Oh, my sister lives there. What's your major?"

Sheesh...pick one. It was probably better to stick with what she knew, though, not the hundred subjects Chloe had studied. "Music."

"Really?" Nancy sounded amazed, which caused Moira a moment of uncertainty. "Pretty different from trick riding, isn't it?"

Uh-oh. Moira nibbled at her lip. She'd very carefully doctored Chloe's résumé to leave that tidbit off so it couldn't trip her up. Unfortunately Chloe's reputation surpassed both their expectations.

"Trick riding?" Bethanie piped up. "You mean where you stand up on a horse while it's running?"

Moira thought she could feel Dutch's attentiveness beside her, but maybe she just imagined it because she was on the brink of trouble. "Well—"

"And where you crawl around in front of its chest to the other side?"

Moira's smile felt as weak as her knees used to get

watching Chloe do that. "I haven't done that in a while." Try *never*. She scooted her chair back and rose for a quick escape. "I, uh, forgot the salt. Does anyone else want anything while I'm up?"

Dutch's hand landed gently on her arm. Her traitorous legs refused to lead her to safety.

"Salt's right here on the table," he said, and set it in front of her plate.

"I...I meant pepper."

"It's right here, too."

What could she do, except sit back down and be glad they were all treating her like anyone else? She had no choice but to sprinkle pepper on her food and hope the conversation did not return to trick riding.

"Did I hear there's a square dance tonight?" Dave asked.

"Sure is," Dutch replied.

"But I don't know how," Nancy said.

"No problem," Dutch assured her. "The wranglers all do. They'll dance you through it like you were born knowin'."

Dave grinned. "Yeah, but what about us men?"

Dutch smiled broadly in Moira's direction. His eyes twinkled merrily. She forgot to breathe.

"We've got female wranglers, too, you know. And our new riding instructor's from Texas."

Unless he was going to ask her to play the fiddle, she sensed big trouble brewing.

"She should be pretty fair at hoofin' it."

Yeah, right!

MOIRA RETURNED to the dorm after supper only to find every other resident crowding the bathroom, all in various stages of getting ready for the dance. Some were doing their makeup, others their hair. Still others were trying on clothes and borrowing earrings.

"Hi, I'm Gina," a long-haired brunette said with a rueful smile. "Come on in if you can find space."

With a shy smile of her own, and against her better judgment, Moira squeezed into the room with the rest of them. It was the only way to reach the showers. Slowly, carefully, trying not to touch anyone, she eased her way through the pack, saying a quiet hello to everyone as they introduced themselves.

"Anybody here got dibs on Wade tonight?" The redhead who asked was sitting on one sink, her foam-lathered legs on the adjacent one, a razor in her hand.

At least five young women laughed and demanded that there were no dibs allowed on that particular wrangler.

A tall, willowy blonde came out of the shower room wearing a short pink robe. "Shower's open if anyone needs it."

"My turn." The brunette who claimed it dropped her robe as she stepped through the doorway.

Facing someone's bare butt was more than Moira could take. With a quick about-face, she waded back through the crowd and fled to her room. She'd shower later. Much later.

THE TABLES AND CHAIRS were pushed aside for the evening's activity, transforming the dining hall to a dance hall. Dutch called the first two square dances, liberally interspersed with instructions for all the willing beginners. There was a lot of laughing and squealing as guests turned the wrong direction and collided, but generally the staff kept most everyone going the right way. They were a good bunch of kids, hired for their attitudes, personalities and general willingness to go the extra mile.

He kept a lookout for Chloe, but she was nowhere to be seen. Apparently she hadn't understood this was part of her job. He handed the microphone over to his head wrangler to do the honors.

As he crossed the square to the girls' dorm, the beauty of the starlit night slowed his pace and filled his heart with contentment. Music flowed outside from the Saloon now, but later there'd only be night sounds lulling him to sleep in his lodge across the valley. He could live on this ranch the rest of his life and love every minute of it. Yessir, now that he had money, he thought—no, he *knew* the grass was definitely greener on his side of the fence.

As he neared the dorm, a break in the music enabled him to hear Chloe's soft, low voice through the open window as she murmured something to her dog. Truth be told, he didn't give a fig about her not being present to dance with the guests. He wanted the honors himself, wanted to hold her hand, rest his fingers at her waist and lead her around the floor.

He entered the dorm, straightened his hat on his head, tucked his shirt in smoother and rapped on the first door on the left.

She opened it promptly, with nothing more than a lemon-yellow towel wrapped around her from breasts to thighs. "Oh!"

His thoughts exactly. Her damp towel was so short, he was afraid to lower his gaze. Instead he focused on how her blond hair, falling loose past her shoulders, was darker now that it was wet. And how the fresh scent of lilacs surrounded her. Not nearly as much fun as looking at her curves and bare legs, but definitely safer territory.

"I...I thought it was one of the others." She clutched the towel at a spot over her sternum. "This is a *girls'* dorm, you know."

"I came to get you. You're supposed to be at the dance to help out. It's—" he had to clear his throat before his voice squeaked like a puberty-stricken teenager in lust "—part of your job."

"I can't dance."

"'Scuse me?"

"I...I stepped in a hole and twisted my ankle."

Against his better judgment, he lowered his gaze to a matching set of trim ankles. "Doesn't appear to be swollen. Better let me have a closer look at it, though." Without questioning his actions, he eased into her room, pressing her backward. When she limped, favoring the right, he reached out and took her arm.

The dog, lying on the far bunk, growled. Dutch didn't need the warning; he already knew he was in over his head.

"Maybe I should get dressed first."

"Nah, I'll just be a minute. Sit on the bunk."

The towel didn't inch upward as she sat—it surged high enough for him to glimpse a tan line on the side, and a faintly puckered scar on the inside of her right thigh. He was both relieved and sorry when, as he crouched in front of her, she pulled a folded pile of white sheets across her lap.

Her ankle was smooth and strong, a perfect ending to a nicely shaped leg. Not a hint of swelling. It took a great deal of effort not to place his hand on her knee and run his fingers up and down all that silky skin. Instead he gently grasped her foot and ankle, bent it up and down, to one side and the other.

"Does that hurt?"

It could have been broken, and he wouldn't have had the presence of mind to know the difference. Now if she'd hollered in pain, that would have been a different story, but she didn't. In fact, she didn't even seem to be paying attention.

"Chloe, does that hurt?"

"No."

Her soft whisper flowed straight to his core. When she tugged her foot out of his grasp, he hadn't the power to hang on to it.

"Just smarts when you step on it?"

"Uh-huh."

He'd had plenty of women throw themselves at him. Was she doing the same, just in a more subtle way? He had to know. He let his gaze wander up her leg, then skipped up to the soft mounds beneath the towel. He was man enough to admit that Chloe was one delicious-looking temptation.

"Anything else hurt?"

She clutched the towel tighter and said, "No," firmly.

He tipped his head, letting his hat shade his eyes and hide his feelings, even though he didn't rightly know what they were. Disappointment?

No, more like respect. He'd had to beat off half the females in Hollywood, and now the first woman he'd had any real interest in didn't capitalize on the unspoken offer he'd just made.

He stood up, then regretted it because he towered over her. "Well, if your ankle's troubling you, I guess you'd better take the night off."

She nodded. "Okay."

He glanced around the small room, seeking a reason to delay leaving. "Need some help making your bunk?"

She shook her head.

"I don't see how you can do it yourself on that sore ankle. Better let me. Here, you move over by your dog."

He didn't give her much choice as he grasped her arms and lifted her to her feet. The pile of sheets landed on the floor, forming a white bridge from her bare toes to his boots.

"No, really, I can do it myself," she said.

He bent to pick up the sheets at the same time she crouched to do it. Her bare shoulder knocked his hat askew. Her towel slipped lower. They both let the hat go and reached for the towel, their fingers tangling over the upper swell of her breasts.

She brushed his hands away and retucked the end in firmly.

"Uh, sorry." Now that he was without his hat, he absently finger-raked his hair. He hoped it fell back into place and wasn't sticking up all over. "Aw, hell, no I'm not."

Her hazel eyes were as soft and curious as a fawn's, and he seized the golden opportunity. He leaned in ever so slowly, tilted his head and gently touched his lips to hers.

They were warm and soft and tasted better than any honey he'd ever eaten. He felt, more than heard, her whisper his name against his lips. He wished her fist weren't clenched on the towel between them, like a rock between their chests, but he wasn't about to brush it aside just yet. She'd move it in her own sweet time.

He traced her lips with the tip of his tongue. He whispered her name. ''Chloe.''

Why that made her start, he couldn't imagine, but she dang near jumped out of his arms.

''Chloe?''

Her face a mask of confusion, she backed toward the growling dog. ''You...uh...you'd better go now.''

Totally confused by her mixed signals, he massaged the back of his neck. ''I'll just make your bunk first.''

''No!''

He was sure he looked as dumbfounded as she sounded stern.

''I'd really like to do it myself,'' she insisted.

''But, I—''

''Really. Myself. Just me. Okay?''

He retrieved his hat from the floor, settled it on his head and debated whether he could grab one last kiss. Between the dog's escalating growls and his innate good manners, he decided against it. ''Couldn't be more clear.''

I'M NOT READY FOR THIS.

With trembling fingers, Moira reached up and traced the trail Dutch's mouth had blazed across her lips.

I might never be ready for this. She stared at the door, which he'd closed firmly behind him. At least he hadn't slammed it.

Ten minutes passed before she realized, probably with a very goofy smile on her face, that she was sitting on the bunk beside her very unhappy, quietly rumbling dog.

No, not her dog—*Chloe's.* Chloe's name, Chloe's history. Chloe had enough of the latter to know how to deal with a man like Dutch. Moira had only her wits to guide her—and they tended to shut down whenever he was near.

As she got up and sorted through the bed linens to figure out what went where, she realized she had to keep her mind on business if she didn't want to be found out as a fraud. She was here to teach Dutch's daughters and the dudes how to ride safely.

While she did that, she was going to learn to be like everyone else. That included being able to make her own bunk, which, after repeatedly tucking the flat sheet under the mattress, perplexed her as to how her staff had always gotten the sheets so taut.

It also included learning how to cope with the opposite sex. If that meant Dutch, in her case, she was going to be a very attentive pupil.

THURSDAY MORNING, Dutch and the guests waited at the corral for Chloe, who was late for the third day in a row.

"Sorry," she said with the sweetest smile when she jogged through the gate, which Tim, who seemed to like his job a whole lot better this week, held for her. *He* hadn't been late for one of her lessons yet.

Dutch thought Chloe, in curve-hugging tan jodhpurs and a purple tank top, looked delicious enough to replace breakfast. But not quite. "You're late again," he growled.

Her cheery smile remained firmly in place. "Are you sure that's an alarm clock on my dresser?"

"Yes."

She shook her head. "I must be electronically challenged or something. I can't seem to get the hang of it."

"Work on it." He strode out of the corral, leaving the lesson to her.

He'd hired plenty of college kids as trail guides to lead the dudes through the scenic San Juan National Forest, but the guests didn't jump at the opportunity. At least the men didn't. Their kids were ready to go. The women, too. In fact, most rides that went out were made up mostly of those, and a few men who'd been married long enough to know what was good for them.

Ben, the drive-in guest who'd made MaryAnne suspicious, was one of the men who attended lessons on a daily basis.

Dutch leaned on the top rail beside his sister. "Office work taking care of itself?"

"Yep." MaryAnne's eyes rarely left Ben, though she kept her hat tipped low and her head turned to the side a little.

"What the hell's that wrapped around his thigh?"

"Who?"

"Don't play dumb...the man your eyes're glued to."

Her momentary silence confirmed it. "I overheard him say he pulled a muscle."

"And he used duct tape?"

MaryAnne's sigh was wistful. "Now *that's* a real man."

"Uh-huh, well, I'm thinking *he's* not the obsessive one on this ranch."

She snorted. "Yeah? Since when do you have mornings to stand around and watch lessons?"

Touché.

He kept his mouth shut and watched as Chloe walked alongside a rider for a moment. She touched his calf with one hand, the toe of his boot with the other.

"Heels down," she reminded him.

She walked beside another rider, then another, giving each one attention in turn, touching a knee here, an ankle there. Her directions were always gentle and concise. She moved them up to a trot, then a slow lope. When those elicited all manner of beginner bounces, she lined them up and demonstrated, with bumps and grinds, how to roll their hips with the horses' gait.

Dutch heard a low groan. When MaryAnne snickered, he realized it had come from him.

"You were right." She added salt to the wound. "Tim's working out after all."

Dutch glared at everyone as they watched Chloe roll her hips forward and back. Forward and back. It didn't ease his mind any that the women were as intent on learning this technique as the men.

"Chloe..."

MaryAnne laid her hand on his arm and said quietly, "Don't cause a scene, little brother. These guests pay my salary."

He made a show of glancing at his watch. He pasted on what he hoped passed for a smile. "Better let these folks go so they can get a swim in before lunch." He opened the gate. "Boys, help 'em with their horses."

"Yessir!"

Under cover of guests dismounting and handing their horses over to the wranglers, Dutch moved in and grasped Chloe by the elbow. As he edged her away from everyone, he said, "Let's get you out of the sun for a few minutes."

"The sun's not bothering me."

When she turned her head, her ponytail whipped beneath his nose and filled his nostrils with the now-familiar scent of lilacs in spring.

He pulled her into the shadows. The air might have been cooler there, but his temperature had risen dramatically from the moment he'd touched her arm. The feel of her soft ponytail brushing against his cheek hadn't helped any. "You need to cool it in front of the guests."

She looked up at him as if he had two heads. "What?"

"You know." He executed a few bumps and grinds of his own. When he saw her look down at his hips, he felt blood drain from his face. That or he had sunstroke, which was pretty unlikely this early in the day. "You don't need to flaunt yourself in front of the men like that. You're making the women jealous."

She laughed lightly.

"If you make them mad, we won't be getting any repeat business next year. I'm serious, Chloe." He could tell by the golden highlights dancing in her eyes that she wasn't. "What're you laughing at?"

"Who're you kidding, Dutch? The women were all looking at *you*."

The only thing that kept him from stammering a denial was the fact that, if the women had all been staring at him—which he doubted—then Chloe had obviously been watching them watch him. And that was half a step in the right direction.

"WHERE'D YOU GROW UP, Chloe?" Nicole asked during the twins' afternoon lesson. It was only her twentieth question in ten minutes.

If everyone else followed the twins' lead in accepting Moira as just an ordinary American grown-up, her fantasy was well on its way to coming true. If only she could have her own bathroom and two extra hours of sleep each night.

"In Texas." She'd always loved Chloe's stories of growing up on a ranch with temporary foster-care brothers that came and went with great irregularity. It wasn't a "normal" family, per se, but had provided Chloe with camaraderie, freedom and warm memories that Moira could only wish were her own. "You're posting on the wrong diagonal."

Nicole turned her attention to correcting that, but, as usual, Katie took up right where her sister left off. "Do you have a mom *and* a dad?"

"Nope, neither. I was raised in a foster family."

"What's that?"

"Heels down, Katie. Oh, wait a minute. Pull up. Your cinch is loose."

Katie stopped her buckskin by Moira and pulled her leg up in front of her on the saddle. Moira lifted the fender to tighten the buckle, only to find there was none. Unlike the cinch on Chloe's Western saddle, this one was tied. Chloe'd never taught her how to *tie* one.

Maybe it's on the other side. She walked around and peeked beneath the off fender.

"What're you doing?" Katie asked.

"Just checking."

"Hi, Daddy," Nicole called out.

Great. A witness to my ignorance.

"Wanna see me ride?" Katie asked him. "Hurry, Chloe, tighten it."

Think, Moira. Think!

She didn't have to look over her shoulder to see how close Dutch was getting. She could feel him, feel his gaze run down her back, over her hips. Making a show of adjusting her ball cap and ponytail, she stalled.

"Got a problem?" he asked, his voice deep as mountain shadows and smooth as silk. Which didn't help her thinking any.

"My cinch is loose, Daddy." In her eagerness to show off her progress, Katie bounced in the saddle. "Hurry, Chloe."

She lifted the fender again, hoping the tie had miraculously turned into a buckle. It hadn't, of course, so she fumbled with the latigo.

"What's wrong?" he asked. "Your hand hurt?"

Sounds good to me. "Yeah, I got stung."

"Good thing you heal fast."

"Huh?"

He glanced toward her paddock boot, then made short work of tightening Katie's cinch. "I notice your ankle hasn't given you any trouble since the dance."

"Oh, yeah."

"Here, let me look at your hand."

She whisked both of them behind her back.

"No, Daddy—"

"—watch us."

"In a minute, girls. Chloe might have a stinger in her hand still."

"No, I don't." Whatever she did for the rest of the summer, she knew she had to quit coming up with excuses that involved body parts. Specifically *hers*.

"You're sure you got it out?"

She nodded.

"Watch—"

"—Daddy!"

Moira tipped her head in the girls' direction. "They've been working really hard."

He took the hint and turned toward Katie and Nicole. "I'm watching, girls."

"It's nice you came to see."

"I didn't, actually." He flashed her his killer grin and said, "But don't tell them. I came because one of the cook's staff got beat up in a bar last night, and we're shorthanded. I need you to help out in the kitchen."

"I can't cook!" She was appalled at how quickly that slipped out. She'd barely ever seen the inside of a kitchen, other than to pour herself an occasional glass of juice or consult with a chef.

He chuckled. "You don't have to cook. You just have to lend a pair of hands."

She wondered if she could fake temporary blindness. But he'd probably want "a closer look" at that, too, and she didn't think her knees would hold her up if he stared deeply into her eyes.

Who was she kidding? Just the thought of him getting that close again was nearly enough to drop her in an undignified heap at his boots.

Chapter Four

Dutch's mountain lodge, built of native timber and stone, originally as a wealthy man's summer getaway, sat high on a ridge where its expanse of windows overlooked a deep valley. In the daytime, the mountains in the distance faded into a blue blur. At night, only two lights could be seen—signs of other ranches tucked away in the hills.

"Bedtime, girls."

Katie and Nicole whined in unison. MaryAnne had told him months ago that this was typical childhood behavior—get over it. He regretted missing the first seven years of their lives. Thanks to his ex-wife's lie by omission, he hadn't known he had any children, much less twins. Once he did know, it had taken him months to get custody. "Get over it" was a difficult task, because he wanted to give them everything he'd never had—especially quality time with a father.

"But, Daddy, we gotta see—"

"—more about the princess."

"What princess?"

They pointed at the television. "The princess of Ennsway."

He'd been watching the same show with them. It

was a special two-hour broadcast on what some people considered the wedding of the century: Queen Moira of Ennsway and King William of Baesland, two small European monarchies. No princess in sight.

"I think she's a queen."

"I'd rather be a princess," Nicole said haughtily.

"Queens are old," Katie agreed.

Moira had been a queen before the wedding, but he let Katie and Nicole have their fantasies. He didn't think she looked a day older than Chloe, either, but knew there was no reasoning with eight-year-olds on age.

In five minutes, the special was over. None too soon, as far as he was concerned. He carried his daughters up the stairs to the bedroom they shared, Katie over one shoulder, Nicole wrapped around the back of his waist. Both were giggling so much he didn't think they'd get to sleep anytime soon.

"Did you see that castle—"

"—and her wedding dress?"

Yeah, he'd seen the castle. He'd gotten more than enough of how royalty lived. Hundreds of rooms, hundreds of servants, museum-quality artwork...it was enough to renew all his old doubts about where the grass was actually greener.

He dumped Katie onto her bed, Nicole onto hers. They giggled as only a pair of eight-year-old girls could.

He glared at one of them, which was hard to do because she'd stood up and was now bouncing up and down on the mattress. "Okay, who are you?"

The other tucked her chin against her chest and tried to talk in a low, fatherly voice. "—and what have you done with Katie?"

Dutch sighed. "You've done it again, haven't you? Okay, swap beds."

They hopped across the floor. "Did you see the horse—"

"—the prince gave her?"

"He's a king."

"But kings are old. Did you—"

"—see it?"

A flashy Andalusian mare. Yes, he'd seen it. It was the only thing the king and queen owned that he'd want. He'd give it to Chloe; the two of them would make one heck of a pair doing stunts.

"Will you girls tell me something?"

"Sure—"

"—Daddy. What?"

"Why did you swap places tonight?"

"So we could be someone—"

"—else."

"But why?"

Katie glanced at Nicole, who studied her stuffed unicorn intently.

Dutch sat on Nicole's bed and leaned back against the headboard. "You want to be someone else, Nicole?" When she nodded, he gently asked, "Why?"

"Well," she began slowly, then picked up speed. "Katie can grow up and be in rodeos and be a rodeo queen. And you got to be somebody else in a movie." She shrugged, then looked up at him with sad eyes. "I want to be a princess."

His need to protect his daughters from old insecurities was strong. "You're as good as any princess," he said firmly. "Better."

Katie bounced over and climbed onto his lap. "Are you as good as a king, Daddy?"

He'd observed King William on the television special. So the guy owned his own kingdom. Dutch's kingdom was this ranch. So the guy commanded respect wherever he went. Dutch had respect—now that he had money, a Hollywood image, and real property. So the guy worked at making life better for his people. Dutch's ranch provided employment for a lot of college kids during the summer, enabling them to earn enough money to carry them through the next school year.

"We think you are—"

"—Daddy." Katie rested her head on his shoulder. "Even better."

He kissed each of them on top of her head. "Thanks, girls."

"Chloe—"

"—thinks so, too."

Their comment was so unexpected that it took Dutch a moment to think of what his next question should be. "Did she say that?"

While he wanted it to be true, he knew it was unlikely that a grown woman would confide in a pair of eight-year-olds, especially twins that jabbered as much as his.

"No, we just—"

"—can tell."

He kissed them again and tucked them in, but his actions had become routine. His mind, so firmly on his daughters for the past year, was centered on Chloe.

Was it possible? Were Katie and Nicole really picking up on feminine signals, instincts that carried from cradle to grave?

He didn't have to worry about whether Chloe

would think he was good enough for her. They were both Westerners, cut from the same cloth. Their interests were horses and the land. Most likely they'd grown up with the same values, except that Chloe thought the twins swapping places was cute.

SUNDAY MORNING FOLLOWED too early on the heels of a week full of late nights for Moira. If being normal/average involved lots of early mornings and an equal number of late evenings, it was going to take her about ten years to adjust.

She'd chosen to live the rest of her life in anonymity, though. The cook did his part. After he'd discovered she didn't know the difference between simmer and boil, he'd scowled at her the same as he would any other kitchen-incompetent person. Ask her to arrange a charity banquet for five hundred people, and she could make it a smashing success. But don't ask her to watch a pot of stew.

She yawned, and stretched until sore muscles screamed in protest. Besides a bathroom of her own, she could use a hot tub. She missed Ludie, the best masseuse she'd ever had. The woman had fingers of gold. Which reminded her...she missed having a manicure, too. In spite of feeling more tired than she'd ever been in her whole life, she wrapped herself in her fatigue and relished it.

She thought, though, that she could do without the pounding in her head. The dog's low growl, as she hopped off the other bunk, pulled Moira out of her fuzzy reverie and alerted her to the fact that someone was knocking at the door.

While she wanted to lead a normal life, it wouldn't

hurt to wish for breakfast in bed, would it? Just this once?

She rolled over, checked the clock and amended her wish to brunch in bed. She raised up on one elbow, brushed her hair back off her face and called out groggily, "Come in."

The door opened a crack, just far enough for Dutch to lean his head and one shoulder in and set Friday to growling. Just enough to make Moira wish she'd combed her hair and washed her face.

"I brought you something."

No, that would be too weird. Besides, she was no longer thinking breakfast. She wanted to see the rest of his chest, the other shoulder. Were they as wide as they had been in her dreams?

"You want to call your dog off?"

"Friday, quit." Amazingly, the dog hopped back onto the far bunk and laid down.

Boot heels thunking as he crossed the wood floor, Dutch strode into the room and parked himself on the foot of her bunk. He crossed one ankle over the other knee and looked as comfortable as if he did this every morning. He'd been dressed the same in her dream: dark hat, pearl-snapped shirt, blue jeans, brown boots.

He looked more delicious in person.

"What? You're looking at me like you expect breakfast in bed or something," he said.

"Yeah, right." She scooted up and leaned her back against the plain wall. She was glad she'd worn Chloe's cotton, baseball-style short set to bed instead of a filmy silk nightie.

He leaned toward her, one hand coming to rest on the mattress near her knee as he held out a piece of paper. She swore she could feel heat off his skin, through the blanket.

"Here, I found this in the Jeep," he said.

What would he feel like, lying next to her?

His low, sexy chuckle only added fuel to her fantasy. "I know you don't want it, but, really, you have to take care of it."

She took the paper from him and glanced at it. It didn't take a great deal of study to remember the speeding ticket from her one and only solo drive.

"Better pay that before they come after you."

Who'd come after me? They would do that? "How do I pay it?"

He chuckled, a cozy sound that made her want to scoot back down in the bunk until her feet rested against his hip.

"You've never gotten a speeding ticket before?"

"Not lately."

"You got a checkbook?"

Chloe had given her hers. Moira nodded.

"Then write a check."

Easy for him to say. She'd never written one except for practice, and then Chloe had stood over her shoulder and supervised. A whole two times. What if she goofed?

"Is there a problem?"

She held firm under his penetrating gaze. "No. Why?"

He shrugged. "You just look like…you might need an advance on your wages?"

She ran her hands through her hair. "It's early, that's all."

He seemed to accept that. Good, she didn't have to

explain she used to wake up to a maid with a breakfast tray, not a hunky cowboy on her mattress.

"You can leave it in the office. MaryAnne'll be sure it gets in the mail. Speaking of which..." He held out an envelope. "You got some."

She couldn't imagine who'd send her anything, until she took it from him and saw the foreign stamps. *Chloe!* Of all the people in the world she might want to hear from, Chloe was at the top of her list. Actually, the only person on the list.

Her best friend had written, and Moira would have to take care that no one else saw this, or her quest for anonymity might be blown to bits. Thank goodness the postmark was blurred.

"Unusual stamps," he said. "Where's it from?"

"A friend of mine's going to school in Europe."

He laughed, rose and eased toward the open door. "Do yourself a favor and don't mention Europe to Nicole. She just saw a TV special on some little country over there. She'll talk your ear off if you get her started."

"Okay."

"I'll get out of here now. It's your day off, so if you see the girls, you'd better hide or they'll pester you into another lesson."

She laughed. "I don't mind. They're really fun."

He smiled in return. "Good. I hope you're liking the guests, too."

"Oh, definitely. Do I do the same thing all summer? Start over every week with the lessons?"

He shook his head. "This week you do the same with the greenhorns, but you get the old-timers—the ones who stayed over from last week—ready for an overnight cattle drive. Speaking of which, I was fixin' to check on the chuck wagon when I found your ticket. See ya later.''

He was out the door and gone before Moira realized he probably expected her to go on the drive, too. He'd expected her to do everything else. Unlike the cook, who hadn't asked her to do anything more difficult lately than set the tables. Even she knew what went where, though it was pretty amazing that people actually ate everything with only one fork per plate.

Putting plates and flatware out was a far piece from roughing it, though—something she'd never done. Heck, she'd never been near a cow, other than milk and steak. In the movies, she'd seen that they kicked up a lot of dust and stampeded over wagons.

Moira's private secretary, Emma, had gone to Ennsway with Chloe to help her over the rough spots. All Moira got was the dumb dog. In her first month as a commoner, she'd sat in a modest apartment in Dallas—nothing too tricky there—and answered ads for employment. She'd concentrated on equine-related work, never imagining that any job she landed would add cows to the equation.

She needed to call Chloe and find out if there was anything she really, absolutely, positively had to know about cows.

By four o'clock that afternoon, Moira had discovered that the only phone on the dude ranch was in the office, MaryAnne was still in there, and Dutch and the guests wandered in and out all day long. She'd heard there was another phone at his lodge, but that was certainly unavailable to her.

Chloe's letter contained both good and bad news. The good news was that she wanted her dog back. Personally Moira couldn't wait. She'd ship her out on the first plane available, but Chloe was sending a jet the following weekend. Seemed now that she was queen, she was making the rules.

Good for her.

The bad news was that Moira's younger brother Louis had grown up to be quite a jerk and had been deported. Chloe wasn't usually given to exaggeration, but still, Moira had difficulty believing he'd actually tried to kill Chloe. That he'd coerced someone to drop a chandelier on her and to blow up one of the towers with her in it.

Moira really needed to talk to Chloe. So much so that she strolled into the office under the guise of being bored and hung around, chatting with a very talkative MaryAnne until Ben came in. Then MaryAnne didn't have time for her anymore, which was just fine.

She picked up the phone and quietly placed a collect call to Baesland-Ennsway.

She leaned against the wall, hoped MaryAnne felt she had enough privacy to carry on a nice, long conversation with Ben, and waited. And while Moira waited, she took note of a few flirting lines from MaryAnne, who was doing a darned good job of it.

When she finally got connected to William's castle, apparently where the queen was in residence at that time, Moira was told, "I'm sorry. Her Royal Majesty has retired for the evening."

"She won't mind if you wake her up for me."

"I'm sorry." The condescending woman didn't sound sorry at all. "That is not possible."

"Really. Just tell her it's...um...Chloe. She'll be glad to talk to me."

"Perhaps if you call back during the day."

"Damn it, you insolent lackey, you put me through to her—"

Click.

"—right now!" Moira didn't have to turn around to know that Ben and MaryAnne were staring at her as if she'd grown horns. Slowly, silently, she replaced the receiver in its cradle and turned to face them. "Uh...sorry."

MaryAnne's customary smile was nowhere to be seen. "This is a family ranch, Chloe. None of the staff uses that kind of language."

She didn't think it would carry any weight that she never had before, either, except in her native language, which no one here would understand. "Sorry. It won't happen again. Is there a library nearby?"

"We have one in the loft above the Saloon. Lots of novels, some encyclopedias. What are you looking for?"

Information on trick riding, square dancing, cattle drives—things I'm apparently supposed to be well versed in.

"Nothing special. I thought I'd just brush up on some..." What was one of the subjects Chloe had studied? "Geology." Yeah, that sounded good. She was in Colorado now. Mountains. Lots of rocks.

"Hmm, you'd have to go into the city for that, but the library's closed on Sundays."

Terrific.

"Maybe I can pick something up for you later in the week, if you can tell me what to look for."

"Oh, that's okay. Browsing's half the fun anyway."

MaryAnne's attention settled back on Ben. Moira strolled outside, stepped off the porch and wandered down the hill toward the barn. There were a lot of new faces, smiling, friendly, as yet untanned. Fresh dudes. As green with horses as she was with her new identity.

By the time she reached the barn, she knew what she had to do. She'd spend the day hanging around with the wranglers, both male and female, who hadn't carpooled off to the city already. Surely they'd discuss the cattle drive. Surely some of them, fresh-faced college kids that they were, hadn't been around animals all their lives. They'd ask questions of the others; she'd listen to the answers. All she had to do was hope they didn't ask *her*.

Then, later that night, it would be daytime in Baesland-Ennsway. She'd be able to sneak into the office and call Chloe.

DUTCH SPENT HIS DAY on the go, moving from one task to another. He welcomed the new guests. He jawed with the old-timers—including Ben, who seemed like a nice enough guy in spite of Mary-Anne's dire warnings last Monday about him being a stalker. He doctored horses, ate lunch with Katie and Nicole and spent a couple hours on the other side of the ranch where he ran the cattle operation.

He wanted to spend part of the day with Chloe, without sharing her. Every time he saw her, though, she was talking with the wranglers. The group was disproportionately male. She smiled at the cowboys, laughed at what those young pups probably thought was wit.

Easy, Dutch ol' boy. They're just kids.

College-age kids, though. Boys who thought they were men. They were built like men on the outside, sounded like men to the ear, flirted like men in the presence of a pretty lady. They were several years younger than Chloe; she couldn't be interested in them.

Could she? And what was it to him? Jealousy?

When he realized that, he wished he had a pile of wood that needed chopping. Anything to work off some steam. After stewing about it for hours, he could only come up with one solution to get *her* away from *them*.

She'd said she liked the twins and wouldn't mind giving them a lesson today. He'd arrange it. Pronto.

TIM SADDLED KATIE'S buckskin while Moira hovered nearby with Nicole's white gelding. He was a talkative young man, so much so that he didn't seem to think twice about how intently she watched him tie the long latigo to the cinch ring.

So that's how it's done. If possible, when Katie was done riding, Moira planned to undo it and see if she could retie it by herself.

Dutch and the twins were late for the lesson, which was no big deal. She'd spent the entire day in more company than she was used to. In a group, without people knowing she was—used to be—royalty, they sometimes tended to talk all at once, over each other at times. It made conversation difficult to follow, generally just at the moment when someone had something to say about cattle drives that she needed to hear.

She watched Dutch walk down the hill, his long, loose stride abbreviated on the slope. Katie and Nicole hopped next to him, ran circles around him, gazed up at him, laughed with him. They frequently reached out and touched his hands, his rear pockets, his belt, as if they needed the connection. He tugged each one's long braid, occasionally picked one up and carried her upside down. It was so quiet, Moira could distinguish his deep laugh and their bubbly giggles.

Even from a distance, she caught their mood. "Careful," she teased when they drew close. "I hear the boss gets grumpy when people are late."

With Katie and Nicole climbing onto their mounts, Dutch closed the gap between Moira and him. When she'd glanced in his direction from time to time earlier in the day, he'd appeared preoccupied, harried. Now his smile was open, his posture relaxed. It was obvious he truly enjoyed time spent with his little girls.

He sidled up beside her and slung his arm across her shoulders.

Her stomach turned a cartwheel.

In the past week, she'd become well aware that Dutch and his girls and MaryAnne were a very hands-on family. So what exactly did this mean?

If he weren't so close, so casual, maybe she could think it through.

"Yeah, gotta watch out for the boss. Hey, girls," he called out as they rode into the corral, "what do you say to Chloe for giving you a lesson on her day off?"

"Thanks—"

"—Chloe."

With his arm across her shoulders, Moira only had the presence of mind to figure out one thing. She'd spent the entire day in the company of men. Not one of them, in all those hours, affected her the way Dutch did in a heartbeat. Even when he wasn't touching her.

Katie crawled to her knees in her saddle.

Moira snapped out of her daze and out from beneath Dutch's arm. "Hey, whoa, wait a minute. What're you doing?"

"I want to learn a trick."

"Break your arm is more like it. Sit down."

Katie obediently sat down and resumed her warm-up. Nicole, looking sad, halted her horse in front of Moira.

"What's the matter, Nicole?"

"Katie can be a rodeo queen when she gets big, but I can't."

Moira smiled up at her. "But you can be in the Olympics."

"I can?"

From Nicole's wide-eyed expression, Moira deduced she didn't have to explain what the Olympics were.

Katie joined their small circle. "She's sad 'cause she can't be a princess."

Dutch uttered, "Uh-oh," just above her ear.

Reminded of how Chloe used to want to be a princess, too, she laughed. "You can pretend to be a princess, Nicole."

"Like the one on TV?"

Moira glanced up at Dutch. "The news?"

"Some European royalty special."

"Okay, girls, how about we get back to your lesson?" Moira gestured for Katie and Nicole to get moving. "Otherwise we'll be late for supper."

Dutch said, "Moira."

"Hmm?" she responded, whirling around to face him before she realized she wasn't supposed to answer to that name anymore. "I'm sorry, I couldn't hear you over Katie. What did you say?"

"Her name was Moira—the queen on TV."

Chloe, a.k.a. Queen Moira, had been on TV? Egads, what next?

"She used to be a princess," Katie added.

"If I was her, I'd still be a princess," Nicole proclaimed.

"Nu-uh," Katie said. "Not if you married King William."

Moira barely heard their banter over whether Chloe had become a queen before or after she'd gotten married. Dutch didn't have his arm around her anymore, but he'd ducked down and was peering beneath her ball cap into her eyes.

"You okay?" he asked.

She blinked.

"You don't look so good. Maybe you've been in the sun too long today."

She forced a smile. "No, I'm fine. Just hungry, that's all." She turned back to the twins, who were still babbling about the TV special as if she'd heard every word. If she didn't cover up better, Dutch was going to ask questions. "Okay, rodeo queen, pick up a trot. And you, princess, start posting."

Both girls giggled and moved up to a trot.

"Chloe, do me a favor, okay?" Dutch asked.

"Sure." She was glad her voice didn't crack.

"Don't encourage Nicole's wanting to be a princess. They're different than us, you know?"

She turned slowly and studied him. "Who? The twins?"

"Royalty. They're not like us."

Interesting. "How so?"

He rubbed his hand over the back of his neck. Then he studied the cloudless sky. "High falutin'. Wealth beyond anyone's imagination. They live in castles. They own whole countries, for God's sake."

She folded her arms across her chest and cocked her head as she stood in the dusty corral and tried to figure out what he meant. "Do you think they're better than we are?"

"Daddy says no one's—"

"—better 'n us."

"They're just people," Moira said.

With his head tipped and his hat shading his eyes, Dutch's expression was indecipherable. "Yeah, with blue blood."

DUTCH FOUND CHLOE in the kitchen late that evening. For a short while, he leaned against the doorjamb and watched her wipe down the ranges. "This is supposed—"

She whirled around, eyes wide, ponytail flying, hand over her chest in a classic startled posture. "Oh! It's you."

He grinned and meandered into the room. "Sorry, didn't mean to make you jump like that. This is supposed to be your day off."

"Yeah, well, you'd better hire somebody quick to help the cook if I'm going to get any more days off."

"I'm working on it." He took the sponge out of her hand and tossed it into the sink. "I think you deserve a reward for going above and beyond. How about an ice-cream sundae?"

She headed for the door. "You don't have to ask me twice. I've got a craving for Chewy Chocolate with Chunks o' Cherries."

"Whoa, hold up."

She turned and walked backward, but she didn't stop. "What?"

"Your apron."

She reached behind her and tugged, but didn't have it undone by the time he caught up to her. Lightly grasping her shoulders, he spun her around and tackled it himself.

"You've got a knot."

"Can you get it out?"

"Just give me a minute." Having his knuckles brush against the tiny bumps of her backbone didn't make the job any easier. He wanted to trace the knobs all the way up, pull out her ponytail and run his fingers through her hair. "Got it."

As he followed her out the door, he laid a hand on her shoulder. It was a natural gesture for him; par for the course. He supposed it had something to do with overcompensating for many years as a loner.

It didn't feel on par with anyone else he'd ever touched, though. Nor did she react the same as anyone else. Katie and Nicole and MaryAnne always touched him back. Buddies gave him a friendly punch in return. Chloe, however, gave him a shy, sweet smile, then ducked her head as if she were embarrassed.

He left his hand where it was and steered her into the General Store and behind the counter. "Let's make our own."

"Okay."

He chuckled and got out a matching pair of old-fashioned sundae glasses. "You don't sound too sure about this. Never made your own before?"

"Can't say I have."

"Well, come on. Vanilla or chocolate?"

She caught her bottom lip with the tip of her teeth and gave the choice entirely too much thought, as far as he was concerned.

"I believe I heard you mention chocolate." He scooped generic ice cream—no "chunks o' cherries"—poured on the hot fudge and shoved both glasses along the counter until they rested in front of her. "You do the whipped cream. I'll find the nuts and *whole* cherries."

He set the can on the counter beside the sundaes. By the time he found everything, plus the twins' stash of colored sprinkles, she still hadn't squirted the whipped cream on top. In fact, she was reading the directions and struggling with the tamper-resistant cap.

He wrenched it off. She returned to the directions.

"Shake it," he said.

She shook her arm as if she were swatting mosquitoes.

"Like this." He demonstrated shaking technique without touching her.

She imitated him.

"Now turn it upside down and push the—over the ice cream!"

She giggled, a light, all-grown-up, not-playing-any-games giggle. "Sorry."

"Okay, now push the nozzle. No, sideways."

"Like this?"

"Watch it." Too late, he had a fluffy ribbon of white stuck to the front of his shirt.

Laughter bubbled from her. "Oops, sorry." She reached out a finger and scooped off enough to taste. "Mmm, good."

"Great." He could only wonder how she'd look with it on *her* chest, but since they were in a public place, albeit empty at the moment, he couldn't very well find out. "How about some on my sundae?"

"Sure."

She squirted his sundae while he wiped off his shirt. The fact that she played with the can as if she'd never held one before wasn't lost on him. He'd thought maybe she'd squirted him on purpose to tease him, but now he wasn't so sure. She seemed more…innocent than that.

Nah, not possible.

He had to know. "We could take the whipped cream back to my place," he suggested in what he considered a rather irresistible, come-hither tone.

"Where's that?"

"About ten minutes through the valley, up to the ridge."

"Wouldn't our ice cream melt by then?"

One look at her face, and he knew he'd been right the first time.

"Oh," she said suddenly. Her cheeks pinkened. She set the can down on the counter as if it had burned her hand.

He waited patiently, hoping she'd agree, hoping she wouldn't.

Whoa! Why the hell not?

Because he liked to think her innocence was for real, that she wasn't as jaded as the actresses who'd begged, bribed and stolen their way into his room at night.

She scooted the can in his direction and picked up her sundae. "I think I'll, uh, eat this outside."

''Yeah, me, too.'' He peered through the open doorway. ''Stars should be out soon.''

AT MIDNIGHT, Moira was still mulling over Dutch's opinion on royalty. Both because it happened to pertain to her and because it was less complicated than visions of him covered in whipped cream.

I'm really not ready for that!

First she needed to learn to cope with his casual touching. Then the heat of his kisses. *Then* maybe she'd be ready for whipped cream—say, around the turn of the century?

She dressed in a dark sweatshirt, dark jeans and pulled on Chloe's cowboy boots. Even with two pair of socks, they were still too big, but she thought she'd blend into the night a lot better if she was dressed like everyone else.

She wrote out the check for the speeding ticket—which she never would have gotten in the first place if she were still royalty. Accompanied by Friday, she crept over to the office to mail it—when, in the castle, a footman would have taken it for her.

She glanced over her shoulder, saw no one and grasped the doorknob to the ranch office.

Locked!

She cursed beneath her breath and checked the front windows. Both were locked. The one around the side wouldn't budge, either, but it was dark enough and late enough for her to spend a little time on it. No one would see or hear her.

She stuffed the check into her shirt pocket and grasped the window frame. She pushed upward. Nothing. She rattled it. Still nothing.

''Need some help?'' a male voice cut through the darkness.

Chapter Five

How would Chloe handle this?

It took Moira all of half a second to realize she didn't give a darn how Chloe would've handled the dark lonely night, the strange man sneaking up on her. Chloe wasn't there. *She* was. And for the rest of her life, if she didn't screw up and get deported, she was going to have to figure out the best way to handle things on her own.

She was going to scream her head off if the guy laid so much as a finger on her.

"It's me," he said.

Now that she had time to breathe again, she recognized his voice.

"Ben."

She'd seen him on a daily basis all week, spoken with him in the lessons. MaryAnne liked him, if the way she flirted with him was any indication. Friday's growl indicated she didn't trust him, though her opinion of all adults was so carved in stone as to be worthless.

Moira felt a measure safer. With a little luck, she might be able to talk her way out of looking as though she'd been trying to break in to the office. Which was pretty darned obvious, all things considered.

"You need to get in there?" he asked quietly.

She nodded, short little jerks of her head, which were safer than saying the wrong thing too soon.

"This way."

Curious as to how he would know a way into the building, she followed him under cover of darkness, around the corner to the front door. "It's locked," she whispered.

"No problem." He reached into his jacket and pulled out a small tool.

With great interest, Moira watched him work the lock with practiced fingers. She glanced around the quiet town square, as if she were the lookout.

"Got it." The door swung inward.

"How'd you do that?"

"Hurry up. And leave that mutt out here. I don't want my leg bit off."

Before she knew it, she was in the dark office, the dog was firmly closed outside, and a small flashlight beam darted around the room.

Ben had come prepared for everything.

Moira suddenly realized that maybe her coming into the office with him hadn't been the smartest thing she'd done lately. He seemed okay, if she discounted the fact that he hadn't been totally honest about his riding abilities. Only someone really comfortable on horseback could pretend to be so inept. Why would he do that?

While the flashlight helped him find his way around the room, she looked for a weapon—just in case—in the dark. She felt her way over to the desk and lifted the telephone receiver. She weighed it in her hand, judging how hard she'd have to swing it to knock a man senseless. Especially a man as tough-looking as Ben.

When she turned around again, the flashlight rested on end on the file cabinet, pointing up at the ceiling, casting an eerie circle of light. The door clicked shut as she was left alone in the office. Friday's growls escalated, then faded, signaling Ben's departure.

Moira locked the door, as if that would stop him from letting himself back in anytime he wanted. But for the most part, it would leave her undisturbed to make her long-distance call to Chloe.

She pulled up a chair, leaned back and propped her feet up on an open drawer. It was time for a good, old-fashioned gabfest with her best friend.

Unable to get through on the first try, Moira shifted positions. She leaned on the desktop and prepared to wait awhile. She was tired, but she wouldn't fall asleep. This was way too important.

She'd think about Dutch with whipped cream on his chest. No shirt, just a wide expanse of bare, tanned skin. And his touch. Oh, yes, his touch. That would keep her awake.

DREAMS OF WHIPPED CREAM and Chloe dancing through his head, Dutch lay on his back, the blanket crumpled around his waist, his chest bare. Beads of sweat dotted his upper lip. When a hand landed on his chest for real, he thought he'd died and gone to heaven.

Until he realized the hand was too small and light, and followed by three more. Not even in his wildest imagination did Chloe have four hands.

The mattress jiggled beneath Katie and Nicole's assault.

"Is he awake?"

"I don't know. His eyes are closed."

"Well, open 'em."

"How?"

"Like this."

Katie's and Nicole's hot breath heated his face as their twenty determined fingers poked him in the forehead, pulled his eyelashes and pried at his eyelids.

"I can't get mine open."

"Keep trying."

It was a sure bet these two little hooligans weren't going to give up and go back to bed. "What the heck are—"

They screamed those piercing, eight-year-old-girl screams. Dutch was glad he didn't have neighbors; they'd have called the cops and reported a murder for sure.

"Daddy, you—"

"—scared us."

He opened his eyes and yanked the blanket up to his chin. "What are you girls doing up?"

"It's morning."

"Three o'clock is not morning. It's the middle of the night. And little girls are supposed to be in bed, sound asleep." He hoped he sounded grumpy enough to send them skedaddlin', but they didn't. He closed his eyes and hoped they'd give up.

"We been thinkin'—"

"—about my new saddle—"

"—an' about me learning to stand up on Buck."

Dutch turned on the lamp and cocked one eye as

menacingly as possible. "Little girls who don't sleep don't get privileges."

"We can't—"

"—sleep."

"Would a story help?"

"Is it about—"

"—a princess?"

He scooted up and leaned back against his head-board. "Are horses the only thing you two disagree on?"

"We don't disagree on horses, just on—"

"—how to ride 'em."

"Uh-huh. Okay, once upon a time, there were two princesses. And one night, after all the candles were out and the whole castle was asleep, they got out of bed."

"What were their—"

"—names?"

"Katarina and Nicoletta."

"Dad-dy. We want a—"

"—real story."

"This is a real story."

"But we bet it won't have a happy ending—"

"—like a fairy tale."

"Depends on whether you fall asleep," Dutch groused.

Katie jumped off the bed and took off running. "I'm gonna go get a storybook."

"Aren't you going with her?"

Nicole shook her head.

"What? You don't talk unless you're together?"

"The Princess and the Pea!" she hollered to her sister.

"Again? But you know that one by heart."

"We want you to 'splain how the princess could—"

"—feel the pea under all the mattresses," Katie finished as she returned.

He held out his hand for the book. "Let's read it again and see if we can figure it out."

With one daughter snuggled on either side of him and the book in his lap, Dutch settled in and forgot it was three o'clock in the morning. He'd been totally focused on his daughters ever since he'd learned about them. He was halfway through the fairy tale before it occurred to him that his bed was big enough to hold another adult.

Maybe it was time to look after a little well-being of his own.

MONDAY MORNING, Dutch realized he'd known Chloe a whole week and only kissed her once. And having kissed her once, he wanted to do it again; had dreamed about it, as a matter of fact.

He'd missed a golden opportunity last night behind the counter in the General Store. He could kick himself now. All that was left to do to rectify the situation was to find her and create another opportunity. Pronto.

He knocked on her dorm door. When he got no answer, not even a penetrating growl, he peeked in and saw that she and the dog were both gone. Though it was such a pigsty, it was hard to tell. The woman needed a maid.

For her to be up and gone already, she must've finally figured out how to work the alarm clock. That, or someone else had decided to "make an opportunity" and gotten her up for an early-morning rendezvous. Who knew what arrangements she'd made with one of the wranglers during all the hours she'd spent with them yesterday? A rendezvous in the barn? A predawn ride in the national forest? Watch the sun come up over Eagle Ridge?

Well, if any of those were the case, he had to do a better job at letting her know he was interested. No sense giving those young cowboys the edge. When she showed up for the morning lesson, he'd make it a point to flash her what his agent called his charm-their-panties-off grin.

Until then, he'd catch up on paperwork. MaryAnne had complained that his "In" basket had piled up this past week. Something about him not keeping his mind on business since the new riding instructor had arrived. When he unlocked the office door, he found Chloe curled up, asleep on his desk.

Talk about an "In" basket!

He tiptoed soundlessly over to where she lay, then just stood there and drank her in like a thirsty man. For once she was without her ball cap and ponytail. Her hair cascaded in golden waves over her ear, caressed her neck. He reached out and stroked it, found it to be as silky soft as a kitten's fur.

Through slightly parted lips, she took a deep breath, as if she'd felt his touch. Other than that, she didn't stir. Her cheek remained pillowed on one hand, while the other was tucked snugly between her thighs, probably for warmth. He couldn't help thinking how warm that might be.

In a sweatshirt and jeans, she wasn't really dressed for the crisp morning air. She needed a jacket until the sun climbed a little higher or she got to moving.

He didn't feel the cold, though. Not now that he knew she'd been waiting for him.

Gently, starting at her knee and working upward, he ran the tip of his finger along the outside seam of her jeans. When he reached the high point of her hip, he spread his fingers, fanned them out until his hand cupped her slender curve.

"Chloe," he whispered hoarsely. "Chloe, wake up."

She popped up to a sitting position and grabbed the telephone receiver, brandishing it like a weapon and sending him on a giant step backward. Wide-eyed, her gaze darted around the office, then settled on him.

"Hey, it's okay," he said soothingly. When he knew that she wasn't going to start swinging, he stepped close again, wrapped his arms around her in a snug circle and hugged her against his chest.

"Oh, it's you."

He thought she sounded more confused than the other morning when he'd sat on the end of her bunk. In her ear, he murmured, "What're you planning on doing with that phone?"

"Oh." She tugged it out from between their chests and hung it up. "Nothing."

He chuckled, loving the way her warmth melded with his own. "Good. Getting hit upside the head this early in the day might give me a headache."

She yawned against his shirt, creating a hot spot right over his collarbone. "Maybe you wouldn't sneak up on me again."

"Heck, don't let that scare you. This ranch is probably the safest place in the world. Why do you think I let Katie and Nicole run around like they do?"

She tipped her head up to him. "Dutch..."

Her soft voice and her trusting expression pushed him over the edge. He whipped his hat off and tossed it in the general vicinity of the file cabinet, not caring in the least where it landed.

He didn't give her much of a chance to continue with whatever she'd been about to say. It was clear she hadn't been out on a morning ride with one of the wranglers. She'd been waiting for him, right there on his desk. He tilted his head and feathered light kisses on her temple, working his way over her cheekbone and down to the corner of her lips.

Her skin was so soft, especially for a cowgirl who'd spent years in the sun and heat of Texas.

When her arms slipped around him, when he felt her hands spread tentatively across his back, he responded in the most basic way. Her fingers glided over muscles that had gone too long untouched by a woman who genuinely cared what was inside the package.

He drew her legs off the edge of the desk and eased himself between her thighs. They were chest-to-chest and had entirely too many clothes on, but he relished the moment for what it was. A testing of the waters, for each of them. He scooped his hand beneath the hair at her nape, which left his thumb right over the pulse throbbing in her neck. Maybe throbbing was the wrong word. Anything pounding that fast and hard and erratic had to be…erotic—for him anyway.

"Dutch…" When she licked her lips and tilted her mouth up to him, he answered her sweet invitation. He dragged her hips against him until he was cradled close enough to make himself suffer.

If this didn't tell her he was interested, he didn't know how to get the message across. Invite her to move out of the dorm and into his lodge? Normally the twins slept as soundly as bears in a blizzard.

"Daddy! Daddy!"

Which was more than he could say for them at the moment.

The door slammed against the wall as Katie and Nicole charged into the office. Dutch refused to spring apart from Chloe as if they were teenagers caught by their parents. He continued to hold her tenderly, even as the twins each clamped on to one of his legs.

"Oops," Chloe said with a shy smile.

He grinned, when what he wanted to do was scoop her up and carry her off to...to...

Hell, there was nowhere private to go that wasn't ten minutes away. A *long* ten minutes.

"Daddy, Daddy—"

"—you gotta come outside."

"In a minute, girls."

"No, Daddy, right now—"

"I'm talking to Chloe right now." He'd be sure to get a few words in so that wouldn't be a lie.

"—'cause there's a dead man in the bushes."

Chapter Six

Reluctantly Moira let Dutch slip away. It wasn't all bad. She got a nice view of how his jeans hugged his hips and pulled taut across his thighs when he bent down and grabbed his hat off the floor. How he towered over Katie and Nicole as he followed them out through the office door. How he lightly laid a large hand on top of each one's blond head to slow her down, careful to keep them both with him, and urged them to let him go first—to no avail.

"We'll show you—"

"—he's this way!"

Moira didn't want to let him go. She wanted him to stay, to take her in his arms again, to teach her more about what it meant to be an ordinary, everyday American woman. One who was in-over-her-head attracted to a rugged American cowboy, a man who had the extraordinary ability to make her blood simmer just by grinning at her.

Nor did she want to tag along. She had no desire to see a dead man. Was it Ben? Did she even want to look and see?

If she was the last person to see him alive, would she be blamed?

"Come on—"

"—Chloe!" floated back inside as the girls took a flying leap off the front porch.

Slowly she slid off the desk, missing Dutch's arms around her, missing how he made her insides feel all fluttery and hot. How his kisses melted her and sent rational thought flying out the window. How his chest felt as hard as a wall of bricks, but carried the warmth of his heartbeat just beyond.

Out the door, across the porch to the corner of the building—she didn't even think about where she was going, she just followed the sound of his deep, resonant voice as he talked softly to Katie and Nicole.

Surely he wasn't making them stand there and look at a dead body!

As Moira stepped around the corner, Katie wailed, "But, Daddy, he was—"

"—right here. Honest, we're—"

"—telling the truth this time."

Dutch had been crouched, studying a section of undergrowth, but rose as Moira drew closer. He nudged a broken branch with the toe of his boot. "Someone slept here, all right. But he wasn't dead."

"Oh, thank God," Moira said in a rush. Relief welled up in a carefree laugh. "It was probably Friday. She followed me here last night."

Dutch shook his head and pushed his hat back a notch with his thumb as he continued to look at the surrounding ground. "Spot's too big."

What did that leave? "A bear?" she asked nervously.

"It was a man and we—"

"—saw him!"

Ben.

"You sure you didn't recognize him?" Dutch asked the girls.

"We told you—"

"—his hat was over his face."

"Uh-huh."

"What was he wearing?" Moira asked.

"A hat—"

"—an' a jacket—"

"—an' boots an' jeans."

Moira glanced at Dutch's amused grin and realized he'd probably already gotten the same nondescript reply. "What color jacket?"

"Brown."

She was determined to do better. "Like a ski jacket?"

Katie and Nicole both shook their heads, each one sending her long braid whipping back and forth like a straw-colored lariat. "Leather."

Moira couldn't think how to pin them down better than that.

"Okay." Dutch bent down to their level and engulfed them both in a group hug, kissed each on the forehead, then steered them in the direction of the square. "You girls run along and find MaryAnne. I'll see you at breakfast."

Katie suddenly clutched his hand. "We're scared of dead people, Daddy, 'specially—"

"—ones who walk."

His face was a study in patience. "He wasn't dead, girls. Just sleeping."

"Promise?"

"I promise." When they gazed at him doubtfully, he asked, "Have I ever broken a promise to you girls?"

Moira thought he looked pretty pleased with himself, as if he knew the answer before they did. As if he'd never broken a promise to them. Not like her own father, who'd promised to summon her home to Ennsway after a short "vacation" in the United States, but never did. Who'd promised to talk with her often, but after a few months, rarely called at all.

If her mother had been alive, she would've made sure Moira returned home, but Katie and Nicole didn't seem to need a motherly figure for an advocate. They were doing just fine with their dad on their own.

They were shaking their heads, verifying what she already suspected about Dutch, that he was a man of his word.

"See how important it is always to tell the truth and keep promises?" he asked in a very fatherly tone of voice. "Now, you know you can trust me. So go on and find MaryAnne."

Katie and Nicole were barely out of earshot before Dutch turned to Moira and swallowed her up in another embrace. "Where did we leave off?" he murmured.

The speed with which he changed from fatherly to sexy devil made Moira's head spin. It definitely made her heart swell, gave her a womanly confidence she hadn't thought she'd feel for years yet to come. It was time to become who and what she wanted to be.

"Trying to figure out who—or what—slept out here last night?" she teased, letting every bone in her body soften as she leaned into him. She didn't have to wonder if she was doing it right; Dutch's gaze smoldered.

"Morning, boss," Wade said as he strode by,

sporting a grin and an unusual preoccupation with the sky directly overhead.

Her cheeks hot with embarrassment, Moira ducked her head, which only put her face closer to the open V above the top snap on Dutch's shirt. While she was quickly growing accustomed to being touched by him—was in fact craving it more than she thought she should—she wasn't comfortable with an audience.

Dutch's fingers curled beneath her chin, gently tilting her face up to his. "I don't believe it." His dark eyes held a definite playful twinkle. And heaven forbid, when he grinned like that, she was bare inches from a dimple just to the right of his lips. "You're blushing."

She made herself look away before she gave in to the urge to press her mouth against that dimple. Out of the corner of her eye, though, she could see that he wasn't making fun of her, that he seemed...proud of the fact that she was innocent enough to blush. His bad-boy grin was sexy enough to make her wonder just how red she was...and what he was up to.

"Well, a cowboy can always give a lady a little privacy," he drawled in a most gentlemanly tone.

Removing his hat, he held it at just the right level, sheltering the sides of their faces from the next passerby as he dipped his head and claimed her lips once more in a kiss so hot, so powerful, that Moira found herself clinging to his shirt—and everything in it.

"How's that?"

"Mmm?" She wondered what it would be like to get really private with him.

Friday grazed their legs as she flew by in a flash, headed for the twins.

Dutch's frown was as unexpected and unwelcome as a cold shower. "How long were you in the office?" he asked softly.

Not sure whether the truth was a wise choice for her at the moment—and not being one hundred percent focused on anything except the kiss they'd just shared—she shrugged offhandedly. "Hours, I guess."

"I don't like it. I don't like it at all."

"I won't do it again," she said demurely. *I won't fall asleep and get caught again, anyway.*

"Not you." He replaced his hat, then cocked his head to one side. "How did you get in?"

"The door was open." *After Ben unlocked it for me.* "I needed to make a phone call, but the line was busy, so I waited. I guess I fell asleep."

"Well, while you were asleep in there, someone else was waiting out here—for you."

"For me?" She wasn't too thrilled about Ben waiting for her, either. Why would he let her into the office and then hang around?

"That's what I don't like. Have any of the wranglers been giving you trouble?"

Feeling braver by the minute, she ran her fingertip tentatively along the open V of his shirt. She smiled, then ducked her head to hide it from him. *Just one. And I wouldn't call it trouble.*

"Chloe?"

"Uh, no, no trouble."

His arms were warm and comforting as he continued to hold her snugly against his chest. His chin drifted across the top of her head, making her hair tingle all the way down to the roots, and she knew he was surveying the surrounding area, a male guarding his own territory.

"Well, just the same, I don't want you wandering around alone at night anymore."

She wasn't too fond of the idea, either, though she still needed to talk to Chloe in private. "Okay," she whispered against his soft chambray shirt, though she didn't consider it a promise. She couldn't.

She visualized him in place of where his desk had been earlier—beneath her. She snuggled her cheek against his chest and imagined it pillowed there for hours on end, with no one to walk by, no one to see.

She might not have any personal experience with men, but she understood the basics. It was all these crazy feelings, the butterflies, the palpitating beat of her heart, the weak knees, that caught her off guard.

"Right after the morning lesson, I want you to pack your bags and move out of the dormitory."

Her head shot off his chest, but his arms held her firmly within their circle. "You're firing me?"

His chuckle was deep and reassuring. "No way, lady. In case you haven't noticed, I've grown kinda fond of you."

"Oh." *Was that a commitment?*

"You'll be safer in my lodge."

"You said this was the safest place in the world." Snuggled in his arms, she felt like it.

"For everyone else, yes. But I won't be able to sleep knowing someone's following you around. This way I can keep an eye on you."

"You mean protect me?" Suddenly his grin wasn't so wonderful and the twinkle in his eyes lost its appeal.

"Among other things."

Her mind racing a mile a minute, she wiggled her

way out of his embrace. ''Dutch, I can't move in with you.''

''Why not?''

''I don't want a bodyguard.'' *Never again.*

''I won't be—''

''I don't need an escort.'' *I want to be like everyone else!*

''I won't be—''

''Or anything else you want to call it. I won't do it, Dutch.''

''Can I get a word in here?''

She folded her arms firmly across her chest. ''Sure. As long as it's 'never mind.'''

DUTCH SLUMPED in his desk chair, shuffling paperwork around the desktop, muttering to himself until he annoyed his sister.

''What's eating you?'' MaryAnne asked.

'''Never mind.'''

''Then quit muttering to yourself over there. You're distracting me and scaring the guests again.''

''No, I mean she said I had to say 'never mind.'''

''Uh-huh, right. I'll just pretend I understand and get back to this schedule.''

''I told her I wanted her to move in to my lodge, and she said I had to say 'never mind.'''

''She said no?''

''She said no, dammit. Now how am I going to keep an eye on her when she's here and I'm there?''

MaryAnne snickered.

''Quit that.''

Her snicker blossomed into full-fledged laughter.

''Hey, cut that out.''

''Face it, Dutch. The staff treats you like a king

and the guests worship the ground you walk on, but I'm your sister, remember?''

"So?''

"So, as your big sister, it's my duty to point out to you that you're acting like a horse's behind. A woman doesn't want to be asked to move in so you can 'keep an eye on her.' She wants to be asked to move in with a man because he loves her.''

He shuffled more paperwork. "I *like* her.''

"You lust after her, little brother.''

He cleared his throat, raked his fingers through his hair, thought about making a quick escape, but her desk was between his and the door.

"If you want to impress Chloe, you won't do it by acting like you're doing her a favor.''

He stared at the mess he'd made all over his desktop. The same one Chloe had slept on for hours. He'd really rather have her curled up next to him in bed where he could get his arms around her and feel her heart beating against his.

"Okay, how do I impress her?''

"That's for you to figure out.''

"You're not even going to give me a hint?''

"Sure, little brother. Figure out what you've got to offer, then play up those good points.''

IMMEDIATELY AFTER Katie and Nicole's morning lesson, Dutch caught up to Chloe outside the corral. Once MaryAnne had told him to play up what he had to offer, everything made sense. He was damned proud of his daughters, but he couldn't offer them up like chattel.

He was also damned proud of his ranch. He'd bought a run-down spread, invested money, time, and talent, and turned it around in the first year. Cordwin Ranch was now a working dude ranch, offering the best Colorado had for a fair price.

With that point firmly in mind, he'd spent hours trying to figure out how to impress her with all he owned—he, a cowboy who'd grown up on the wrong side of the tracks—and finally came up with a plan.

"Chloe, I need someone to trailer two horses over to the far side of the ranch." Let her make that scenic drive alone and see just how much he had to offer. "You just volunteered."

"I can't."

That wasn't the response he'd planned for her to make. One thing about Chloe, he never knew where he stood. "You've stepped in another hole? Doesn't matter. The truck's automatic."

"No, I—"

"Another bee sting?"

"No..."

The determined scowl on her face made him think he'd better let her get a word in edgewise, so he clamped his mouth shut and waited.

"I was going to say that you already lent me to the cook, if you recall?"

"He'll have to do without you today. My foreman needs these horses pronto. Now, it's a pretty far drive, so I've drawn you a map. Though if you get lost, you'll be on my property nearly the whole time—" he thought he'd slipped that in quite well "—so we'll find you eventually." He grinned for further effect.

She shrugged. "Okay."

He wished he had a hidden camera in the cab of the truck. He'd like to see the expression on her face when she saw just how much land he owned. That'd knock her socks off for sure. Dammit, it still impressed the hell out of him. Imagine what it would do to a simple cowgirl who'd grown up in a foster family.

He glanced around, saw no one was looking and patted her on the fanny. A mistake, he discovered, as soon as he realized there was something a whole lot more personal about skin-tight jodhpurs than stiff denim. The sultry look she aimed up at him was a whole lot more personal than he'd hoped for, too.

"Where are they?"

"Where's what?" *Geez, that's real impressive, cowboy.* "Oh." He pointed toward the barn and handed her the keys. "Trailer's over there. Take the truck next to it. Horses are in the first two stalls."

Slowly could best describe the speed with which she took the map from his hand. He didn't think it had anything to do with the tingle he felt when her skin brushed his.

Her eyebrows puckered delicately. He thought about kissing the wrinkle away, but then he wouldn't get her out on her own to see his side of the mountain.

"You want me to hook up the trailer?" she asked.

He nodded.

"And load the horses?"

"That's generally how it's done. You can handle that, can't you?"

"Oh, yeah," she said lightly. "Just checking."

She turned and walked away, giving him a long, leisurely view of the soft sway of her hips. He wanted to shout after her not to take all day, but hell, he was enjoying it too much.

The truck and stock trailer were fairly new and in excellent condition; he wanted to be sure to give her plenty of time and space to notice that. He was proud of all he'd acquired since he'd made that movie. It had earned him a lot of respect. Even MaryAnne respected him, though she'd never admit it. Why, she'd probably sneak off to town to see it rather than let him know she knew it had premiered the day before yesterday. His agent had sure pitched a fit when he'd been ''too busy'' for all that hoopla.

He meandered around the barn area, covertly watching Chloe. If he impressed the heck out of her with the size of his spread, would she admit it? Or would she be like his sister and make sure success didn't go to his head?

He wondered if that king—William, was it?—had used the size of his kingdom to woo his queen.

Nah. It was downright ridiculous to think a king would have real-life problems.

After ten minutes, he wondered how, for a Texas cowgirl, Chloe could have so much trouble getting the truck backed up so the ball lined up with the hitch. He hoisted a sack of feed to his shoulder and strolled in her direction, arriving just as she booted the rear tire of the truck with a good, swift kick.

He grinned. ''First you ditch my Jeep—''

She whirled around.

''—now you're assaulting my truck. Why do you have it in for my vehicles?''

She smiled sheepishly. ''I didn't hear you coming.''

He glanced at her dog sitting in the truck. ''She tried to warn you.''

''Yeah, well, I've gotten so used to her growling, I don't even notice anymore.'' She turned back to the truck. ''I don't think I hurt it.''

"No, I don't think so, either. What's the problem?"

"I...I can't get it lined up."

"So I see. Why is that?"

"I...I'm used to a gooseneck. It's a lot easier to line the hitch up when it's right there in the bed."

"Ah." He supposed that made sense. On the other hand, he doubted she'd *always* had a fifth wheel. "Well, I've got a minute. Why don't you get behind the wheel again and let me guide you back?"

He didn't have to ask twice. She climbed into the cab, held the door open with her hand on the window frame, drove a few feet forward, then shifted into Reverse.

"Okay, come on back. Slow now. Easy." *The way I'd like to make love to you.* "A little to the left. Too much—back the other way. Don't rush it." *Yeah, me, too.*

She leaned her head out. "How am I doing?"

He'd whip off that damned ball cap and pull her ponytail loose first. Let her hair fan out across his pillow.

"You're almost there. Another six inches." He cleared his throat. "Two more. That's it."

"Am I under it?"

"Yeah, it oughta slip in just fine now."

"Great!" She slid down off the seat and bounced back to him. "Thanks. I couldn't do it without you."

He shifted the heavy sack to the other shoulder. "That's what I'm hoping."

"Huh?"

"Oh, nothing. You did fine."

"You want to show me how to get it on?"

Oh, yeah.

"Dutch? Are you all right?"

"What? Oh, yeah, I'm fine."

"You look like you're a million miles away."

"Nah, just about thirty seconds is all."

"What? Never mind. Show me how to crank this onto the ball, okay?"

"Uh, yeah." He cleared his throat again so his voice wouldn't crack. "Grab that handle there and give it a twist."

He watched her small hand wrap around the metal shaft, the sway of her body as she cranked it, the bob of her ponytail as it kept time.

"Okay, it's slipped in. Now what do I do?"

He closed his eyes and struggled to take one deep breath after another. Anything but think about what he wanted her to do next. "Close your, uh...the hitch. And slide forward—the collar, I mean. Slide that forward." With his sleeve, he mopped beads of sweat off his lip. "I gotta go. Can you handle the rest?"

"Put on the chain and plug in the brake lights? Sure. You should go drink something, Dutch. You look like you've had too much sun."

"Inhaled too much of this feed, that's all." No sooner had he turned to walk away than he felt her pat his behind.

This from a woman who blushes?

Although, it *was* kind of a shy, tentative touch. Still, a pat was a pat. He tossed a cocky wink over his shoulder and managed to keep a nice, even pace, but as soon as he reached the shadows of the barn, he bolted for the hose. A cold stream of water over his head and across the back of his neck was what he needed.

Dripping, he peered out again after the horses were

loaded and she was driving away. Smoothly this time. Not like when she'd delivered his Jeep. Apparently an automatic transmission agreed with her.

He'd driven his Jeep after she'd finished with it the day she'd arrived. He didn't think it drove quite right—probably needed a minor check after she'd bounced it across the ditch and mowed down the trees—but there was nothing wrong with the way it shifted. No reason she shouldn't have been able to drive it without grinding the gears.

So what *had* her problem been?

GOOD HEAVENS, WHAT WAS I thinking?

Safely alone, Moira took her butt-patting hand off the steering wheel and stared at it. She squeezed it into a fist and opened it again, testing to see if the tingling dissipated at all.

It didn't.

Giving in, she allowed herself to feel again how his denim-covered behind had felt in the palm of her hand.

Not once, but twice.

Firm. Well-toned. No bulge of a wallet to get between him and her. Nothing else between her hand and his rear.

She looked at Friday. "Is it hot in here?" A mountain breeze blew steadily through the open windows. "Nope, just me, huh?" She flipped on the air conditioner—to the frigid zone—and steered her thoughts to safer territory.

She didn't mind not having to help the cook. She always watched how other people on the kitchen staff did their jobs, certain that, one day, he was going to give her an assignment more difficult than setting places.

She could handle carrying platters of food out to the side table, knowing they were arranged in groups for each of the dining tables, so nothing would be forgotten. Making toast didn't look too difficult, and she wouldn't be the first to scorch a couple of slices.

But if she were asked to make the tea or watch the stew simmer or grate cheese, she'd be in trouble.

Trailering two mature horses, who'd taken one look at the stock trailer and stepped in like old pros, was definitely the better choice. She'd never pulled a load before, but it followed right along behind the truck without any problems. Except for the gate post. How was she supposed to know how close it was on the far side—on a curve—without crawling across the seat and looking out the window? Good thing no one had come along with her. They'd have died laughing.

Dutch's map was easy enough to follow. He'd drawn all sorts of unnecessary items on it. "Scenic view of Eagle Ridge" was labeled with an arrow. It was pretty magnificent, but it was no Swiss Alp.

"Route to prehistoric cliff dwellings" was clearly marked so she wouldn't take that route.

"Acres of wildflowers" caught her attention.

"What is this? A travelogue?" She tossed it aside and enjoyed the scenery without his commentary.

The sky was blue, the few white clouds cast large shadows on open pastures. She rattled across a cattle guard, entered open range and got to see her first steer up close—like next to the side of the narrow road.

"Stay there, buddy. I'm just passing through."

She laughed at the ease with which she slipped by him, afraid he was a bull and would charge. *This* they didn't have around Ennsway Castle. *This* large, docile creature represented all she'd been protected from her entire life. He hadn't even blinked at her. The only animal that had ever hurt her had been a dog, which hadn't hurt as badly as her father sending her to American doctors and forgetting about her.

The blare of a horn from behind caught her attention.

"Okay, okay." She gently pressed the accelerator.

The road was too curvy for her to go much faster, considering her inexperience with a load and open range. In her side mirror, she glimpsed an old green-and-rust pickup, weaving back and forth, trying to find its way around her.

"Keep your hat on, buster."

The horn blared again. It was at a moment like this that she severely missed being a princess with a limo driver. He'd know what to do, and his knuckles wouldn't be turning white. She refused to go any faster. It just wasn't safe. He'd have to wait.

When she reached a comparatively straight section, she hugged the side of the road so he could pass, but he rode her bumper instead. So she sped up, and he kept pace with her.

Until the next curve, when he shot around her and cut across her left front fender. Reflexively, she turned the wheel sharply to the right. She missed him, but she missed the rest of the road, too. She headed over the embankment, with a lot of weight pushing from behind. Like a film rolling before her eyes, saplings appeared to rush at the hood of the truck, only to suddenly disappear as she plummeted downward.

Where the heck are those trees going? was quickly replaced with *Please, let the horses be okay.*

And *Damn, I never got close enough to Dutch.*

Chapter Seven

Worry gnawed at Dutch like a fly pestered a horse. Someone had gotten comfortable in the undergrowth outside the office. Someone who'd followed Chloe? Nothing like this had ever happened on his spread before. It was a nice, family-atmosphere dude ranch where people came to vacation, relax and forget the crime statistics. He was lucky to be able to offer that to the guests.

Who would've thought he'd also get lucky enough to hire a woman who overcame her shyness just long enough to pat his behind and make his blood boil?

"So who do you think would sleep in the bushes and wait for her?" MaryAnne asked across her desk.

He raked his fingers through his hair. "I don't know. Wade maybe?"

"Nah, too young."

"Tim?"

"Too lazy."

He shook his head. "Not anymore."

She snickered. "You just don't want to fire him."

"He's starting to work out all right. He gets to every lesson before she does."

"Yeah, and then he disappears."

"But not until the lesson's over and the horses are taken care of. I'd say he's got a thing for her. Maybe he was following her and fell asleep."

"You're jumping to conclusions, little brother."

"Now why the heck would I do that?"

She grinned and sounded quite innocent when she said, "I don't know, Dutch. Why would you do that?"

He didn't give her question the consideration she so clearly wanted. "Okay, smarty-pants, who do you think it was?"

"My vote's on Ben."

"Ben?"

She rolled her eyes like a teenager. "How many times do I have to tell you? He's not a dude."

"Looks like a dude. Darn near fell off his horse at a lope this morning like a dude."

"It's an act."

He scowled. "For a grown woman, you sure are ignorant."

"What's that supposed to mean?"

"If he's acting, it's just to get your attention."

"Is not."

"Is so. You've been making cow eyes at him, too."

"I'm just keeping tabs on him, since you won't."

"Uh-huh."

"Hey, if Chloe ends up missing, don't say I didn't warn you."

His gut reacted with a quick kink. "Don't say that. Maybe it was her dog after all. Or maybe Katie and Nicole lied to me again."

"They don't lie, Dutch."

"The hell they don't."

"They're not like their mother. Oh, they tease you once in a while because you're such an easy target, but they don't lie. I believe someone slept out there, and I think it was Ben. He's always near where Chloe is."

"So? You're always near where he is."

"Well, I'm not now," she said with a huff.

He narrowed his eyes for a closer inspection. "Why is that?"

She shrugged as if it meant nothing.

"Couldn't find him, huh?" The kink twisted into a definite knot. "You don't know where he is?"

"Nope."

Hair prickled the back of his neck. Common sense told him to ignore it. Something deeper wouldn't let him. "She should be on her way back by now. Call the foreman and see how long ago she left."

He had to wait a long ten minutes for a portable phone to reach his foreman. When the connection was finally made, MaryAnne's frown told him more than he needed to know. He surged to his feet.

"She hasn't gotten there?" she asked over the phone. "You're sure?"

He slammed his hat on his head and yanked the door open. "Tell him to start looking from their end. I'll drive over from here."

SLOWLY, Moira opened her eyes to find everything tilted at a crazy angle—very disorienting until she took a few deep breaths and let the dust settle. She finally figured out it was the truck, fifteen feet down a boulder-strewn hill, which was askew, and not the world.

A check in the mirror reassured her the stock trailer

was still behind her and a tad more upright than the truck. Personally she thought the hill was a little too steep for her to not have both feet firmly planted on terra firma. From the sound of shod hooves kicking the inside of the trailer, the horses felt exactly the same way.

She glanced out the window for help, hoping someone competent would be in the area checking cattle or something. No such luck.

Where's a cowboy when you need one?

Only one she wanted to see right now sprang to mind—Dutch. And he wouldn't be anywhere nearby. He'd be back at the dude ranch, thinking his horses were in good hands with Chloe when, in fact, he'd sent them off with a princess who hadn't a clue what to do now.

If someone told him the truth, he'd get that little scowl he wore sometimes, a wrinkle right between his eyebrows. The first time she'd seen it, he'd been afraid she was going to back his Jeep into the ditch.

Then his face would light up with his sexy grin, as if he thought someone was trying to put something over on him.

And finally, when he realized she really was a princess, he'd take Katie and Nicole firmly in hand and repeat that "they're different than us, you know?" line of his. He'd take his precious little girls and walk away.

Her only consolation at this point was that anyone could have been run off the road. Even the most seasoned driver.

With a dirty look in Moira's direction, Friday scrambled from the floor back onto the seat. When Moira reached out a reassuring hand, the dog not only

growled, but she also pulled her lip back and showed
a full set of pointy teeth.

"If you hate me so much, why the heck did you
come along?"

She'd drugged the dog and crated her for an air-
plane ride. There'd been that little mishap with
Dutch's Jeep. Now this. Undoubtedly Friday would
be ecstatic to see Chloe's jet next weekend.

It would also be an opportunity for Moira to throw
herself at Chloe's feet and beg to have her identity
back. What did she know about being a cowgirl, anyway? Crashing a stock trailer definitely wasn't what
she'd had in mind when she'd asked to trade places.
Of course Chloe was married to King William now
and quite unlikely to take mercy on Moira's predic-
ament.

She wouldn't mind Dutch riding up just then on a
white horse and taking charge. Except the only white
horse in the near vicinity was trapped in the trailer.

Moira knew what she had to do—sort of. With the
angle the truck was on, and as shaken as she was from
the accident, she couldn't push the door open. She
crawled up and out through the window.

"I'm coming," she said in the most soothing tones
she could summon up for the horses' sakes. She stumbled over the rock-strewn slope, caught herself and
continued to reassure them with more assurance than
she felt. "Easy now."

If she concentrated really hard, she could imagine
she heard Dutch saying the same things to her. He'd
been in her thoughts all week, whether she was having trouble being a cowgirl or carrying it off successfully. She knew exactly how he spoke, loved his
deep baritone. Loved how she felt all tingly whenever

he was near. Loved the way he could reach out and touch her so casually, so confidently, so tenderly.

"Easy, fellas."

She looked at the slope, studied the trailer and decided, whether she thought she could do this or not, she had to. She talked to the horses a bit more, climbed up on the running board and peered in at them. At least they were on their feet. Lucky them—they had four each to balance on, so they'd be better on this hill than she was.

When they saw her, their feet moved as quickly as their ears. As they shifted, the trailer slipped a foot downhill. "Great."

It didn't take long to find a rock to block the wheels; it did take a while to pry it out of the ground with her bare fingers and wedge it next to a tire. After that, her head starting to clear, she quickly and calmly entered the trailer and led the horses out one at a time.

"You guys are good as gold," she said as she patted their sweaty necks.

A streak of red blood on a white foreleg caught her eye. The gelding wasn't too happy about her inspecting his gash, but it had to be done so she'd know how serious it was. She scoured the inside of the truck and trailer for a first-aid kit, but found none. The only thing she had to bandage him with was her tank top, which she whipped over her head without hesitation. It wasn't like she was standing out on a city street in her bra. The only things around her with eyes were the horses and a few curious cattle.

And the cop who drove up right after she had her lime-green top tied around the horse's foreleg, sopping up crimson blood. She dodged to the far side of the gelding, so all the cop would be able to see were her feet and her head.

On the edge of the road above her, he opened his door slowly, stepped out and asked, "Speeding again?"

She saw red, and it wasn't the horse's blood. "You've got a radio in that car, don't you?"

"Yes, ma'am."

"Then notify Dutch to get on over here and bring some bandages."

"You hurt?"

"No, but his horse is."

"God, lady, first his Jeep, now one of his horses. I'd better hang around and make sure all he does is fire you."

She'd been a princess too long, given too many orders in her lifetime to miss this opportunity. "Call him!"

It felt great.

DUTCH FELT HORRIBLE.

Ever since MaryAnne had notified him that Carlson had called in with Chloe's whereabouts, that there'd been an accident and help was needed, he'd been driving like a madman to reach the site. To reach her.

He'd sent her off with a truck and trailer in an area of the mountains that she didn't know. Forget that she'd grown up traveling all over creation from one rodeo to another. Forget that the weather was clear, the day sunny, traffic nonexistent. If she was hurt, he was to blame.

He skidded his Jeep—which now drove so poorly after the "Chloe incident," he realized it *had* to go in for repairs—to a halt right behind Carlson's patrol car. He'd drawn a really simple, clear map for her to follow.

How the hell had she gotten way over here?

Standing on the edge of the road, he looked down the slope and scanned the accident. His gaze sped over the tilted truck, the crooked trailer, the two horses standing peacefully munching on a bush.

When he saw Chloe on her feet, talking to Carlson, obviously uninjured, he drew in a breath so deep it hurt his lungs.

He covered the terrain down to her with more speed than good sense, considering the rocks, boulders, and fallen tree trunks that could have tripped him up. Any one of them could have flipped the truck and sent it and the trailer rocketing all the way to the bottom.

Could have sent her with them.

He threw his arms around her. "You okay?" The first time Katie had fallen off Buck, he'd discovered that caring for someone was hard work. Now, with Chloe, he thought it might take years off his life.

She was warm and whole, thank God. The scent of lilacs filled him, reminding him of spring and new beginnings. When her head nodded against his chest, he squeezed her a little, afraid she might have sore ribs or other injuries. When he got no complaints, he tightened his hold. Then it dawned on him—

What the heck was she doing wearing a leather jacket in the middle of a hot afternoon?

He held her at arm's length, took a closer look and fingered a lapel. "What's this?"

"Oh—" she smiled shyly "—Carlson lent me his jacket."

"You tore your shirt?" It was the only explanation

he could think of. And that meant— "You're hurt? Are you bleeding?"

His hands flew over her, squeezed her arms to see if any bones were broken, unzipped the jacket. Maybe she needed compresses or stitches. Carlson turned away and averted his eyes as Dutch acted on pure instinct, on reflex.

Until he pulled the jacket open to see the prettiest, laciest bra he'd ever laid eyes on. The lime green shade only served to remind him that was the very color her tank top had been earlier—when she'd been wearing it.

Underwired, it offered him plenty to look at. Low cut, it showed the swells of her breasts. Perfect mounds that would fill his palms. Cleavage that begged him to bury his face in it.

"What the hell—" She shot away from him, tripped over a boulder, landed on her behind and rolled toward the horses' feet.

Dutch saw leather, skin, and lace, all in a revolving blur. She was unhurt—before, anyway—and he had a lot of apologizing to do. Right after he helped her up and found out what had happened to her shirt and why she was wearing Carlson's jacket. And how much of her bra *he* had seen.

"Freeze!"

Rushing after Chloe, reaching out for her, caught off guard, Dutch froze.

Carlson brushed past him and helped Chloe to her feet before she got stepped on. "Good thing I hung around," he said pointedly as she tugged the zipper up in short little jerks.

Dutch began, "Chloe, I—"

"Sir, I'll have to ask you to go back up to your vehicle."

"Sir?" Dutch had always liked the respect that title conveyed. Now it sounded cold. So *official.*

"I'm okay, Carlson," she said calmly. "Really."

"I'll see you get safely back to the ranch."

"No, really, he was just—"

"His sister'll look out for you." He glanced at the truck and trailer, and shook his head. "You'd best pack up and leave the state, though."

He tried to usher her up the hill away from Dutch, who admitted he had to give her credit when she dug in her heels.

"No, wait." She slipped her arm free. "He was just trying to—" She pinned Dutch with a glare. "What the hell were you trying to do?"

"I saw the jacket. I thought you might need first aid."

Carlson grasped her arm again. "Yup. Makes a lot of sense to me. Lady's wearing a jacket, you figure she needs first aid."

"Well, hell." Dutch exploded. "It's ninety degrees out here. Why would she take her shirt off in front of you unless she was hurt?"

"She didn't. It was already off when I got here."

Dutch got a vivid image of Carlson driving up and Chloe greeting him in nothing more than that damned wisp of lime lace.

"You thought I was hurt?" Her soft voice was a welcome relief to dealing with Carlson's suspicions.

"I...I thought, if you tore it in the accident, that you were cut. Or something," he mumbled. He was rewarded for his effort when she stepped closer to him. "I thought you might need a compress."

Her gaze never left him as she asked, "What do you think, Carlson? Does he look sincere to you?" Only her smile hinted that she was teasing him.

"That, or he's a darned good actor."

Dutch's gaze was locked with hers as well, as he wasn't about to break it. "I'm a damned good actor—when I'm in Hollywood. So what happened to your shirt?"

She spread her hands on her hips and went on the offensive. "Did you know you have no first-aid kit in your truck *or* your trailer?"

"No, not really," he said through tight lips. "Are you hurt or not? Or do I have to tackle you and rip that jacket off to find out?"

I should be so lucky.

"Your horse is."

He didn't have to follow her pointing finger. The bloodstained bandage against the white hide of his horse drew his eye like a beacon—now that he no longer had to worry about Chloe being hurt. "Is he going to need a vet?"

"Unless you like to sew."

"I'm pretty handy with a needle. I haven't always had money."

"In your pre-Hollywood days?"

He'd barely nodded when Carlson butted in. "I saw his movie last night."

If Dutch knew how to send the man packing, he would have. Not that he minded Chloe finding out he'd made a movie.

The officer's whole demeanor changed to admiration. "He was fantastic. And—" he winked in Dutch's direction "—if my date's reaction is any indication, those Hollywood studs better be lookin' over their shoulders.''

Dutch decided it wasn't so bad having Carlson around after all. He clapped him on the shoulder as if they were old buddies. ''Hey, they're okay guys.''

Chloe's eyes widened.

MaryAnne had told him to sell himself on his good points. Would Chloe like him better as a movie star than a cowboy? And why did that bother him? He was the same person either way. One was as good as the other.

Irritation grew as he recognized old insecurities creeping in. He was as good a man today as he ever was. The only difference now was that he had enough money to take care of a woman, to give her anything she desired. If Chloe wanted a whole dresser full of sexy lingerie, he'd be more than happy to oblige.

It was more important, though, that he showed how he felt about her, how he'd lost ten years off his life when he thought she might be hurt. And he would—as soon as he figured out how. In the meantime, he'd continue to emphasize his strong points.

He unbuttoned his shirt and flashed what his agent billed as a pretty impressive set of pecs. He shrugged it off his shoulders. ''Here. You can give him his jacket back now.''

DUTCH AND CHLOE sat next to each other on the side of the hill, overlooking the truck and trailer, overseeing the horses. At least *she* was watching the horses. He was wondering if the rest of her underwear was lime lace. It was a far more delightful image than wondering who the hell drove the green-and-rust pickup truck she'd described to Carlson and him.

"You're sure you're all right?"

Chloe sighed. "For the hundredth time, yes. Would you stop asking?"

"Sorry, can't."

She looked sexy as all get out in his shirt, with the tails flapping around her thighs. In her skin-tight, tan jodhpurs, it wasn't difficult to imagine her wearing none at all. Visions of a morning after flooded his mind and made other conversation exceedingly difficult.

That, and he was still figuring ways to impress her.

"Maybe you'd like to soak in a warm tub or something."

She nodded. "There isn't one in the dorm, though."

He knew that. He had another plan. Hopefully, one of these times, one would work. Otherwise the summer was going to be over before he'd accomplished anything. She'd head back to school in Santa Barbara, probably, and leave him holed up here for the winter.

When his foreman and crew finally arrived, Dutch gave Chloe a hand up. He was quick to notice she moved slowly and carefully. "I know I'm not supposed to ask, but—?"

"Just stiffened up."

He assisted her into the Jeep by placing his hands anywhere he thought would help—without getting him slapped in the process. When he felt something brush against his leg, he looked down and saw Friday staring up at him. "Yeah, you, too. Get in."

She put her front paws up on the running board and gave him a look more sorrowful than anything Katie or Nicole had tried on him.

"I guess she's sore, too," Chloe said. "I've dumped her onto the floor twice now."

Before the dog could remember to growl at him, he scooped her up and dumped her onto Chloe's lap. "Maybe you'd better hold her this time." After he was behind the wheel, he gently suggested, "You kind of have to put your arms around her to hold her, you know."

Chloe remained rigid in her seat. "I don't think so."

He rested his elbow on the steering wheel and studied the odd picture the two of them made. Not the usual devoted owner/loving pet image. "She doesn't like you much, does she?"

"Gee, I'm not sure," she said with dry sarcasm.

"Why keep her, then?"

She started to answer right away, then gave it more thought. "I promised," she finally said.

"Her?"

"No, someone who loves her."

"Why?"

"Because she's my friend, and she went away to school in Europe, and she knows no one else'd take care of this mutt."

"Yeah, I can see why. She must be a really good friend."

"You have no idea."

He U-turned the Jeep and headed up the narrow, winding road to his lodge, hoping it wouldn't make anyone carsick. Ten minutes later, they rolled through a gate. "We're back on my land now."

When he pulled to a stop in front of his native-timber-and-stone lodge, the dog jumped out, but Chloe didn't.

"Where are we?"

"My place."

She glanced around. Was she nervous? The last thing he wanted was to make her nervous.

"I've got a hot tub out back that you can soak in."

Her eyes lit up for a moment before her expression clouded. "I don't have a suit."

He hopped out. "No problem. We'll have a 'no clothes' rule."

"Great." She allowed him to take her arm and help her out of the Jeep, then tossed the most delicious smile up at him. "When will you come back for me?"

MOIRA STOOD ON THE DECK and looked longingly down at the hot tub. She didn't have to ask if it came with a masseuse; she knew it didn't. Unless, of course, she wanted to ask Dutch for a back rub. Which she did.

And she didn't.

Not that he'd have any problem with it, but she'd just barely gotten up the nerve to pat him on the rear, fully clothed. She wasn't sure she'd come far enough to lay half-naked in front of him and let him run his hands all over her. Though, after having her life flash before her eyes, she was ready to move forward a bit faster.

"I'll rustle us up some food in the kitchen." His tone hinted that he'd rather she change her mind about letting him join her.

"Food sounds good."

Disappointment flashed across his face, then disappeared with a grin that clearly said he wouldn't be a man if he hadn't tried. "Oh, one more rule. No dogs in the hot tub."

She laughed. "I wouldn't dream of sharing it with her."

He inched closer, as if he were going to come right out and ask to share, but then he turned and left her alone.

She stripped down and slipped into the hot, steamy water before he could find a reason to come back. It was hot and bubbly and felt so, so good. Putting her head back, she melted into the preshaped, reclining bench and dreamed of how things used to be. Back when she'd been a princess and enjoyed her own spa every day after riding. Then a masseuse worked out all the knots. A manicurist touched up any nails she'd damaged. If she were going out, her maid styled her hair for the evening. Her clothes would be laid out. Classical music would be playing throughout the condo, filling her with a sense of ease and expectation.

But if things were the way they used to be, she wouldn't have met Dutch. He might not fill her with a sense of ease, but she definitely was getting expectations.

She knew Dutch already had plenty of them. Unfortunately, one was probably that a woman her age had experience in matters more basic to the survival of the species than pinning ribbons on winners at charity horse shows, sponsoring symphonies and hosting banquets.

CHLOE WAS CRYING her eyes out when Dutch returned to the lodge. He'd driven the Jeep back down to the dude' ranch and left it there until the dealer could work it into his schedule, then borrowed MaryAnne's pickup.

A box of tissues sat on Chloe's lap. Several wads of them dotted the hardwood floor at her feet. Tears streamed freely down her cheeks. Her fingers hovered around her trembling lips.

His first fear was that she was in pain from the accident, but when he recognized the music blaring from the television, he realized she was watching Katie and Nicole's copy of "Wedding of the Century," the tape he'd made for them of Queen Marie or Mary or someone and King William.

He slipped onto the far end of the couch without distracting her—a good thing for him because he could sit and stare to his heart's content, if he didn't go deaf first.

Startled, she jumped when she noticed him, and grabbed for the remote.

"That's okay," he yelled over the music. "Let it play."

When the last note ended and the narration returned, she reduced the volume and sighed. "I can't believe she selected Beethoven for the wedding."

"Bad piece?"

When she glanced at him, he got the feeling she didn't even see him. As if he weren't really there.

"No, it was great. It fit the church. You're not in a hurry to get back, are you?"

He shook his head, then faced the television as if he were interested. "I forgot her name. Something real different."

"Moira." She said it softly, almost reverently, and then she captured her trembling lower lip with her teeth.

"Yeah. Moira. Real different. Sounds kind of royal, doesn't it?"

Her head bobbed in a motion somewhere between a nod and a shake. Definitely noncommittal.

"I mean, normal women have names like MaryAnne and Katie and Nicole. And Chloe." When he got no reply, he asked, "Why are you crying?"

"Oh, I, um, always cry at weddings."

"Why do women do that?"

"She's so beautiful." A fresh deluge streamed down her cheeks, and she set to blotting. "Look at her."

He preferred to study Chloe's profile. "You know, you two look a lot alike."

It could have been his imagination, but her spine seemed to stiffen. Her gaze darted from the TV to him. "No, not really."

"Same hair color." If he was going for points here, he could do better than that. "Same nice figure, too."

"Mmm, I think she's taller."

"Well, I know you're prettier." He studied her a little longer, wondering why she was so entranced by the royal wedding in front of her. Was she like Nicole? "Would you like to be a queen?"

She punched the Off button. "Would you like it if I were?"

His laugh was hard. "Hell, no. I told you, royalty's out of my league. If you were a queen, you'd be all snooty and unapproachable."

"Snooty?"

Was that a smile?

No, definitely not. She looked…offended.

He scooted across the cushions. The closer he got, the more he noticed she'd withdrawn, but he pressed on until he was as close as he could be without touching her. "I want you just the way you are, Chloe."

Her smile was tentative. Her eyes still shimmered with unshed tears. "You...you do?"

He nodded. "What the heck would I want with a queen?"

"I don't feel like a queen. How about a princess?"

"Nah. A cowgirl from Texas is more my style."

When he reached out to touch her cheek, to see if it felt as soft as it looked, she shot off the couch. The remote control clattered to the floor among the crumpled tissues.

She quickly fell to her knees and began gathering them. "Sorry for the mess."

He bent over, trying to see something other than the top of her head. "Did I say something wrong?"

"No! Of course not." Her laugh sounded forced. "What could you possibly have said wrong?"

"You seem upset."

She offhandedly waved a wad of tissues in the air. "I'm just...emotional today, that's all. I'm not used to endangering the lives of innocent horses."

Well, she still has her sense of humor.

When she headed for the trash can in the kitchen, he was left to think about where he'd gone off track this time. She denied he'd said anything wrong, yet she'd withdrawn, just like before.

Am I pushing her too fast?

Nah.

He just didn't understand what was important to her yet. MaryAnne had told him to stress what he had to offer, but Chloe knew what he owned, and that hadn't worked. His sister must be off base.

What was Chloe missing in her life? That he could provide?

Well, for starters, she was no longer on the rodeo circuit. Did she miss it? Did she miss the trick riding? The thrill? Was teaching dudes a step down after that kind of life?

Maybe for some people.

If she had a trained horse, would she go back? Because he could do that for her. Buy her a trained horse, ready to go. Not that he wanted her to go, but even if he bought her one, she'd have to spend weeks practicing with it. Months maybe. Right here on his ranch.

It would give her a reason to stay.

Chapter Eight

Dutch loved sing-alongs. He tried to have one after every evening meal unless there was a square dance following. This evening had been no different, except he'd noticed Chloe.

He grinned like a fool. *Well, I always notice Chloe.*

She didn't seem to share his fondness for good music, though. How a cowgirl like Chloe got tangled up with Beethoven, he'd never know. How she could turn her back on classics like "Oh, Susannah," "She'll be Comin' 'Round the Mountain," and "Clementine," he'd never understand. Even "Deep in the Heart of Texas" hadn't gotten her clapping her hands with everyone else.

He didn't know if he'd ever understand her, but there was one thing he could do for her. When he saw MaryAnne head for the office for the final lockup, he burst in after her.

"Get on the phone," he ordered.

She tossed him a distracted frown. "You fired her? Again?"

"Nope. I want you to find a horse for her."

"Okay, sure. None of yours will do, so I'm guessing she needs one with six legs or two heads?"

How she could be sarcastic and distracted at the same time, Dutch wasn't sure, but it brought him to a quick halt next to her desk. "No, the normal number of appendages will be fine. But I want one that's trained for trick riding."

"Well, heck, why don't I just find a pair that's already trained for Roman riding while I'm at it?"

"I'm guessing there's a problem here. You want to clue me in?"

She stuffed her hands into her jeans' pockets. "It's Ben."

"He's married?"

She started pacing, giving Dutch a clue how annoying that was for the one left to watch.

"He's got a gun."

As much as he wanted to get Chloe a horse—yesterday, if not sooner—he had to admit that a guest having a gun on the dude ranch took priority. "What kind of gun?"

She shrugged. "I'm not sure."

"A pistol or a revolver?" *Like it mattered.*

"I'm not sure."

"How could you not know— Never mind. Where is it?"

"I'm not sure."

"MaryAnne—"

"He's got a gun, I tell you! I felt it under his jacket once. And then, later, when I got close again, I didn't. So I don't know what he did with it."

"Where is he?"

"I don't know." She stopped pacing long enough to kick at a desk leg. "He seems to follow Chloe a lot."

"Ah."

"No, not 'ah.' I am *not* jealous."

"Sure, sis."

"Well, what are you going to do about it?"

He wiggled his hat into a more secure fit. "I'm fixin' to have a talk with the man."

"You're not going to beat him up." It was neither a question nor a declaration on her part. It sounded like a concern.

Apparently his big sis was smitten.

"No, I won't beat him up."

"You want me to keep an eye on the girls until you get back?"

"No need. They drug Chloe off to the General Store for ice cream." He grinned. "Though I'm not sure who was doing the dragging."

Sure enough, he found Ben slouched in a chair on the Barber Shop porch, his feet up on the rail, his hat tipped low as if he had nothing better to do than snooze the evening away. His position gave him full view of the General Store entrance.

Was MaryAnne right about him following Chloe?

"Evenin'," Dutch said as he slumped into the chair next to Ben.

"Evenin'."

He put his feet up on the rail, too, and tried to look as nonchalant as a P.I. in a movie. Who knew? He might get a role like this someday. "You enjoying your stay?"

"Yep."

"Going on the cattle drive?"

"Is your sister going?"

Dutch felt a modicum of satisfaction in that he'd called it right; Ben had a thing for MaryAnne, not Chloe. "You interested in my sister?"

Ben pushed his hat back a notch. "Hell, you're not gonna ask me my intentions, are you?"

"Should I?"

"Look—" Ben took a deep breath "—I'm just a guy on an extended vacation, okay?"

"How extended?"

"Most of the summer."

Not many people put away enough money to spend months paying dude ranch rates. Dutch got the feeling MaryAnne might be justified in her suspicions after all. Might as well get right to the point.

"You need a gun on vacation, Ben?"

"I'm a cop. Regulations require me to keep it on me at all times."

"Are you on a case?"

"Nope, I'm just taking the summer to get back in shape."

"Not following anybody?"

"Look, I tore some muscles in my leg." His hand landed on his duct-taped thigh as if to prove his straightforwardness. "I'm just here for some R and R."

"R and R's fine. The gun's not." Dutch rose so that he would tower over Ben to issue his warning. "You hand it over to MaryAnne to lock in the safe before tomorrow morning's lesson, or you pack up and clear out."

MOIRA DIDN'T REALIZE how much she'd been missing music until she'd been enveloped again by Beethoven. Who would've thought Chloe knew the perfect music to pick for the ceremony?

On second thought, it had to have been Emma.

Chloe might know Country/Western, but she hadn't a clue as to classical.

"What are you humming?" Katie asked as she jogged Buck around the arena the next morning. It was their last riding lesson before the cattle drive.

"Beethoven."

"Beethoven's a dog. How can you—"

"—hum, a dog?"

"He's not a dog. He *was* a composer, a long time ago. If you watch that tape again that your dad made for you of Chl...uh, Queen Moira and King William's wedding, you'll hear his music."

"Are you gonna be our—"

"—new mom?"

Amazed at their quick change of topic, Moira couldn't even begin to imagine how the two of them managed to come up with the same thought at the same time.

"We saw you and Daddy kissing yesterday—"

"—outside the office. MaryAnne—"

"—saw you, too."

Personally Moira would rather be kissing Dutch again instead of dodging their questions. "Nicole, change diagonals."

"There'd only be one thing better than for you to be our mommy—"

"—and that's if you were a princess mommy, like Queen Moira, 'cause then we'd be princesses, too."

They still hadn't gotten the princess/queen thing entirely straight. Trust Nicole to know what was important, though; royal titles were hereditary.

"You look like her, too. You 'n' her could trade places—"

"—and fool people just like we do sometimes."

Maybe speed would shut them up. "Okay, girls, move 'em up to a canter."

"A lope." Katie corrected her.

Who cared, as long as they didn't continue on this tack. "Yeah, whatever."

"Would you do that?" Nicole asked.

"What?"

"Trade places with Queen Moira?"

"Why would I want to do that?"

"'Cause the grass is greener there."

Moira laughed. "Do you even know what that means?"

"Yep, Daddy told us and told us—"

"—and told us."

"Well, the grass is green enough right here for me."

"Because you like—"

"—Daddy?"

"It was green before I met your daddy." That was only half true. She'd thought she'd be happy anywhere in the United States. Lately she was thinking it might just be in Colorado.

"Daddy gets real mad when we swap places," Katie said pointedly to her sister. "Chloe wouldn't want to make Daddy mad."

Katie's statement only emphasized what Moira already knew. If she got the opportunity, she ought to help that tape disappear. And she could never tell Dutch the truth.

THERE WAS A SLIGHT DELAY in lunch in the dining hall. The cook was still operating one person short—one competent person anyway. Dutch occupied the dudes with his guitar and another sing-along.

Moira tried to hum as the guests sang. It was that or go out there, wrestle the poor, mistreated guitar from his hands and show him how the instrument was *supposed* to be strummed.

The cowboy could sing, and he might be able to play a guitar, but it was a sure bet he couldn't do both at the same time.

Lunch was ready none too soon for her. She shared a table with the Jefferson family, MaryAnne, and Dutch.

"Miss the girls?" Moira asked him.

He chuckled. "Are you kidding? All I hear is 'When do I get a new saddle? When do I get new riding clothes?'"

"Lucky you."

"There's more," he whispered when everyone else was occupied in a lively discussion of the upcoming cattle drive. "I'll tell you when we're alone."

She figured it was along the same lines as what she'd gotten this morning during the lesson. It was one thing to have the girls talk about seeing her and Dutch kissing; they were children. She didn't know how to handle it if he brought it up, though. Not in words, anyway.

"Looks like somebody's lost," MaryAnne murmured. A young man stood just inside the door—a blond, clean-shaven, Brad Pitt double with a camera hanging around his neck. His gaze darted around the room as if he were searching for someone in particular. "That, or we've got another walk-in guest."

"Looks too touristy to me," Dutch commented. "Guess I'd better send him on his way."

No sooner had he tossed his napkin onto the table and stood up than the man zeroed in. In a flash—

literally—he rushed forward, snapping pictures of Moira and everyone at the table.

She was caught off guard, unable to turn away fast enough. Her ball cap was hung up on a hook, the same as at every meal. She had no protection as her worst nightmare began to unfold.

"Paparazzo!" Moira said with disgust.

How had he known she was here? Had she come this far just to be exposed now? He continued snapping pictures haphazardly—of her, Dutch, the dudes, the children, whomever he could get. As if he'd sort through the results later and pick what he wanted.

"What?" Dutch asked.

The photographer turned and strode for the door.

"Stop him," Moira ordered. She didn't know what she'd do with him, she just knew she couldn't let him take that film away.

"Ah, let him go," Dutch said as he started to sit back down.

With Chloe's image having just been splashed all over the television, and Dutch and the girls—and who knew who else?—thinking she and Moira were look-alikes, Moira couldn't write the man off so easily. She'd dealt with paparazzi since she'd come to this country. She'd learned how to dodge them, how to turn to just the right angle at the last second.

She didn't need her picture splashed on the front page of a tabloid under a caption that read "Look-alike Princess? Or the Real Thing?" She didn't want Dutch labeled as "The Princess's Secret Romantic Cowboy." It was worth anything to prevent that.

She jumped to her feet, sending her chair reeling backward. "Stop him!"

Dutch looked up at her as if he thought she'd lost her mind. "Let him go. It's free publicity."

"It's invasion of privacy, dammit." She darted across the room toward the unsuspecting photographer, who apparently decided if Dutch wasn't going to object, he needn't run away. Until he glanced her coming at him.

He shoved a chair in her path and made a beeline for the door. She stepped onto the seat and took a flying leap for his shoulders. She landed on his back. Realizing she'd just lost her mind and was going to crash onto the floor and probably break every bone in her body, she dug in her fingers, wrapped her legs around him and hung on for dear life.

They crashed to the floor together, where she came out on top and straddled him.

There was no turning back now. "Give me the film."

He laughed up at her. "No way!"

She wanted to smash his avaricious smile. Instead she gritted her teeth and punched him in the chest. "Give...me...the...film."

Dutch towered over both of them, but his hands landed on her shoulders, gentle, yet firm. "Chloe, it's okay."

"Jeez, Cordwin, if I'd known you'd hired a bodyguard," the downed man muttered, "I'd have come better prepared."

"Yeah, well—"

She yanked at the camera. When he wouldn't release it, she pummeled his chest again. Repeatedly.

"Get her off of me!"

Fortunately for Dutch, he didn't. Instead he took a step back. "Or what?"

"Or I'll file assault charges."

"You can do that with two broken arms?" he asked with deadly calm.

Moira fleetingly thought she'd like to see his movie if he talked like that in it.

"This is my film. Not hers. Not yours."

Moira poked him in the throat, wrenched the camera from his grasp and smashed it against the floor. Twice, during which time she noticed a lot of feet had circled them.

"Hey!"

"Allow me," Ben said, bringing his boot heel down on it squarely.

Dutch pushed him aside, picked the camera up and stripped out the roll of film. He sighed. "Well, here's to free publicity." He stretched it out in the daylight, then turned around and grinned at his guests.

"Next time, our feisty little riding instructor'll use a rope to lasso her prey. Wait'll y'all see her on the cattle drive."

The twinkle in his eyes and the smile he flashed her were worth a million-dollar-movie contract in Moira's estimation.

"Better let the man up, darlin'."

The paparazzo scrambled to his feet, keeping a wary eye out for both Ben and Chloe. "I got a right to take your picture, Cordwin. You're a movie star now. Your fans expect to see you."

Movie star? She'd forgotten.

His fans? She'd jumped to conclusions—the wrong ones.

Dutch nodded. "I know that, son." He flashed a sheepish grin that even had Moira believing his sincerity. "But next time, bring a cheap camera."

He put on a good enough show for his guests that Moira began to think he might just be a really great actor, when she knew he must be confused by what she'd done. If so, it didn't show as he urged everyone back to their lunch. She knew he must suspect she was some criminal on the run, yet his smile was open and friendly as he took his place beside her at the table.

"We'll talk later," he said in an undertone.

But Moira knew he wouldn't hear the truth from her. He couldn't; he'd hate her for it.

MOIRA DODGED DUTCH the rest of the day. A cowardly thing, she knew, but she figured the more time between her lunchtime tackle and their "We'll talk later," the more time she'd have to come up with a logical explanation.

Whenever she saw him, she made sure she looked really busy getting ready for the cattle drive, which would leave the next morning. She eventually decided that, if and when he finally trapped her and demanded an explanation, she'd say she did it to protect the children. She'd point out that it was okay for a photographer to take his picture, but his children weren't public property and needed to be protected.

Sounded plausible enough in her head. Of course, she was grasping at straws to protect herself.

Due to the fact that she was keeping one eye open for Dutch all afternoon, she also noticed Ben seemed to be following her. Neither of them had ever mentioned breaking into the office; it was as if they didn't talk about it, it hadn't happened.

That evening, when she glimpsed Dutch moseying her way, she ducked into the General Store.

"It's about time you got in here," MaryAnne said. "If you don't get one of these straw hats, you're gonna burn up on the drive for the next two days."

Moira looked up at the shelf of straw cowboy hats. *Big-brimmed* cowboy hats. Perfect for hiding from unexpected camera shots. She whipped off her ball cap and pulled out her ponytail. "Not a bad idea."

MaryAnne laughed and reached up toward the stack. "Of course not. What size?"

Size? I'm supposed to know this?

She shrugged, and remembered she'd never gotten hold of Chloe for other pertinent information, either.

"Well, here, try this one on."

It slipped down and covered her eyes. "Too big."

"Mmm, I see." MaryAnne handed her another. "Can I ask you a question?"

Oh, Lord, here it comes.

She cocked her head on an angle as if she were studying Moira better. "Are you interested in Ben?"

Moira blinked. "No. Why?"

MaryAnne shrugged and busied herself straightening the stack, leaving Moira to try on another and check herself out in the mirror. Yep, tipped down low, it hid a lot. She tipped her head slightly this way and that, the way she'd done for years with dress hats. This worked just as well, if not better.

"It seems like he's been, well, watching you a lot."

"He has?" Now that she knew it wasn't just her imagination, Moira chewed her bottom lip as she thought about what his motives might be.

"You didn't know?"

"No." She hoped the angels weren't keeping track of her lies. "What should I do?"

MaryAnne seemed to take pity on her. "Don't look so worried. He's not dangerous or anything. He's a cop."

"Oh." She tried to sound relieved, when in fact she now had to be concerned about why the police were following her. Which was a pretty simple guess. She'd finally gotten the check mailed off for her speeding ticket, so it wasn't that. And it wasn't as if someone questioned her signature, because Ben had arrived at the ranch the first day she'd been there.

Had the law found her and Chloe out some other way? Was what they'd done illegal?

Well, I guess!

Now was one of those times when it would pay to be a princess. If she were, all it would take would be a word from her, and Ben would be "dealt with." But she wasn't and she couldn't.

She couldn't risk another call to Chloe, either. Not with a nosy cop following her around.

"Oh, I almost forgot." MaryAnne pulled an envelope out of her pocket. "Here."

"Mail?"

"Nope, it's your paycheck."

Moira took it, stuffed it into her pocket and said, "Thanks," as if she got one every week.

Inside, though, she was jumping up and down, celebrating this milestone in her quest to be average. *My first paycheck!* What would she do with it?

Well, that was easy. If she'd known what a luxury it was to have Yanni or Enya piped through her thirty-room, cliffside condo, she'd have brought a CD player to the ranch with her. Now she could buy one for her dorm room and wake up to her choice of music rather than that blasted clock radio, which was just as likely to greet her with a grisly newscast as anything.

Although...she hadn't a clue how much a CD player cost or if one paycheck would cover the expense.

DUTCH CARRIED KATIE and Nicole to bed, kissed them good-night, read them a story—*The Princess and the Pea* again—and tucked them in.

"One more time—"

"—Daddy."

If they made him read it again, he'd know it by heart. Who ever heard of feeling a pea beneath one mattress, let alone twenty?

He was rescued by the ring of the telephone and begged off.

When Dutch picked up the receiver in his kitchen, his agent roared, "What the hell's the matter with you?"

It sounded like a coffee kind of conversation, so he poured a mugful. "What's up, Larry?"

"Free publicity, man, that's what. And you threatened the guy? What's wrong with you?"

"It seemed important at the time."

"Okay, I'm counting to ten here. Maybe you can tell me why it was important—" Larry began shouting "—to expose the film? I mean, I can understand taking a punch at the guy. They expect that sort of thing. Threatening him, that's okay, too. But dammit, Dutch, it's good publicity to get your face spread around while your movie's hot."

"Hot, huh?"

"Yeah."

"How hot?"

"Number one at the box office this week."

"Gee, you don't think that could be because Gibson directed it, do you?"

"Gibson, Shmibson. It's because you were in it, Dutch ol' boy. Now, I'll tell you what I'm gonna do. I'm gonna talk that photographer into driving back up to your place tomorrow."

"Won't be here."

"You can't pass this up, Dutch."

"I'm taking the dudes out on a cattle drive for two days."

"Even better! Cowboy in action. They'll love it! Remember what I said. You can threaten him. You can even take a swing at him, but don't do any damage, okay?"

"Okay."

"And for God's sake, keep that kamikaze cowgirl off of him."

Click.

Dutch stared at the receiver and sipped his coffee. Kamikaze cowgirl, hmm? He chuckled. Pretty damned good description of Chloe flying through the air. She sure was camera shy. But apparently if she was going to be spending any time around him, which he hoped—after all, he'd made over two dozen phone calls tracking down an experienced trick horse for her—she was going to have to get over that.

Ben had said he wasn't on a case. He'd even let MaryAnne lock his gun in the safe. Was it possible he'd lied, though? That he wasn't recuperating from a leg injury, but following Chloe for legal reasons? That she was hiding out?

She seemed so innocent, downright naive at times,

that he couldn't imagine what the law would want with her.

Unless Ben had lied about that, too. He hadn't flashed a badge. Maybe he was up to no good following Chloe. Maybe MaryAnne wasn't too far off the mark with her stalker theory.

In which case, Dutch resolved to keep a closer watch over Chloe.

Chapter Nine

Wednesday morning dawned bright and clear as the guests met at the barn to van over to the "working" part of the Cordwin Ranch. Unused to getting up at dawn on their vacation, they quickly forgot how tired they were when Dutch pointed out the pinks and golds of sunrise over the mountains. The first trills of the birds were greeted with smiles and a round of toasts with steaming coffee mugs.

"Nice place to live, Dutch."

"Yeah, how do I get me one of these ranches?"

"Does it look like this every morning?"

It did Dutch's heart good to hear those comments and more. This is what he'd always wanted. Respect. Admiration. His guests hadn't even seen his new movie yet—maybe didn't even know about it until the photographer had shown up in the dining hall. They respected him because it was a quality that fed on itself. Once a man had it, it just followed that he got more. From everyone.

Bob Davison, one of the more gregarious of the guests, was a case in point. A big man, he could have easily scared the women and intimidated the men, but he'd seen how Dutch's staff respected him, and he'd turned out to be the teddy bear of the ranch. "Hey, Chloe, where's your rope?"

His to-the-point query earned a hearty laugh all around.

With a smirk, his wife quipped, "Yeah, can you teach me how to lasso? I don't think I can handle that tackling business at my age."

Dutch imagined Chloe's cheeks were a blush of red, but he couldn't tell with that darned cowboy hat she'd donned for the ride. The straw brim shaded her hazel eyes and wouldn't allow him to see half as much face as he used to, or nearly as much as he wanted.

In the distance, a cloud of dust rose as a red pickup sped through the gate. Unlike Chloe, the guys back in Hollywood had a grudging level of tolerance for cameramen as persistent as this one, and that after they'd been photographed for years. More and more just didn't seem to add up right about her.

Not that he suspected she was guilty of anything except attracting a possible stalker.

On his bay gelding, he stopped beside Chloe, who rode the dappled gray mare she'd taken a fancy to. He'd bought her at an auction months ago, hoping Nicole would be impressed, then found out they both needed more mileage before they could be put together. In a week, Chloe had taught the mare more about manners than she'd learned in all her seven years.

"I want to keep the guests with you for the first mile or so," he said. "Let everyone settle in first."

"Okay, boss."

At that close range, he could see beneath the brim to the twinkle in her eyes again. He was tempted to spend the entire cattle drive right there, where he could side-pass his gelding right on over until his knee bumped Chloe's on occasion. She'd never know it was intentional. And if she did...

He grinned. *So much the better.*

She wore jeans and cowboy boots today, a much more sensible outfit for a cattle drive than her jods and paddock boots. Just as sexy, though.

MaryAnne rode up on Chloe's far side, slapped a rolled-up newspaper onto her lap, said, "Thought you two might like to see this," and cantered off in haste.

"What the devil?"

Chloe glanced at him, as if he could explain his sister's behavior. When she unrolled the newspaper, she groaned.

"Let me see."

There, on the front page of the worst rag in the country, was a picture of Chloe taking a flying leap off the dining hall chair. Dutch was a slight but recognizable blur behind and below her.

"'Bodyguard or Babe?'" he read aloud. He winked. "Catchy headline."

The driver of the pickup parked beside the barn and stepped out in clear sight.

Dutch ignored him in favor of scanning the column to make sure his movie was mentioned, but Chloe rolled the paper up too quickly. She slapped it against her thigh like a weapon.

"How'd he get that picture?" she muttered through tight lips.

He wanted to kiss them back to their regular, soft shape. "Don't have a clue. Second camera, maybe? It's pretty funny, when you think about it. Who'd believe a cowboy would hire a little bitty thing like you as a bodyguard?''

As the paparazzo strode closer, Chloe tucked her chin, bringing her brim down and cutting off Dutch's view completely. For that alone, he wanted to horse-whip the guy.

She neck-reined to the side. "I'm going to get Katie and Nicole out of range."

"Katie and— What have they got to do with this?"

She halted just long enough to say, "If you want your picture taken, that's your business. And if you want theirs taken for a respectable article, that is, too. But I don't want a sleaze like that anywhere near them."

Stunned, he sat motionless as she loped away, her dog in hot pursuit. So she'd tackled the guy and demanded he hand over the film in order to protect Katie and Nicole? He wished he had a script for his life lately. He was having trouble keeping the players straight.

Either way, he was rolling his sleeping bag out next to hers tonight.

"HEAD 'EM UP!"

Moira didn't know what the heck that meant when Dutch bellowed it from the back of his gelding, so she led her group of dudes, along with Katie and Nicole, to the far side of the herd. The wranglers all knew, though. Whistles sliced through the air. Masculine voices hollered at the animals.

"Move 'em out!"

Dust, kicked up by hundreds of bovine and equine feet, billowed upward and floated on the breeze. She'd lost track of the paparazzo, didn't know whether he'd been invited to tag along or not. Regardless, it was quite evident that Dutch was on his way to fame for the movie he'd made.

What had Carlson said? *Those Hollywood studs best be lookin' over their shoulders.*

And so should she. If Dutch was going to be followed and photographed often, it would be next to impossible for her to keep working for him and maintain her anonymity. Lately she hadn't planned on seeing him only during working hours. She'd liked him coming to her room and sitting on the foot of her bunk. She hoped he'd invite her to make ice-cream sundaes again—she'd like to have another try at the whipped cream, and not have to get it on the dessert.

A deep baritone broke through her thoughts as it burst out in song. She couldn't see him, but she recognized Dutch's voice. She listened, amazed as everyone else joined in, men, women and children alike, to sing a song she'd never heard of. A lively tune about... *raw* hide?

If they all knew it, right down to the kids, it was obvious she should have come across this somewhere in the past sixteen years, except she'd been too darned sheltered by Emma and the rest of the staff.

"C'mon, Chloe. Can't you—"

"—sing?"

She'd studied a lot of music over the years. Apparently the wrong type. "I don't know it."

"Daddy taught us. We'll teach you—"

"—later, okay?"

It was one thing not to know one song. It was quite another when the exercise was repeated until her head was swimming. The drive proceeded under tunes about fences, big irons on hips, and happy trails, whatever those were.

Dutch rode up to her group, assigned dudes to wranglers and sent everyone off while he and the twins remained by Moira's side. "You don't like to sing?"

She cleared her throat and said in a raspy voice, "Can't. The cows are kicking up too much dust."

"The *cows?*"

"Yeah," she rasped, not sure what she'd said wrong, but knowing it had something to do with the cows.

"Okay," he said quite seriously, "who are you and what have you done with Chloe Marshall?"

Uh-oh, I blew it. I've been found out.

She glanced at the twins, hoping they were up to some mischief to distract Dutch from the inquisition she could feel coming. If their big-eyed expressions were any indication, though, she'd just shocked them as much as she had Dutch.

She could lie—if she could think of something fast enough that sounded good. She could deny that she knew what he was talking about, but it wasn't as if she'd grown up lying and had much experience at it. Or she could explain.

I don't think so.

It was an appropriate time for a coughing spell, she figured. There was enough dust to account for it. Anything to delay the inevitable. Trouble was, when Dutch's hand pounded on her back to help her out, she nearly forgot what the problem was. She was torn between liking his gloved touch and wondering if he'd quit before her eyeballs popped out.

Faking it was the option that flitted into her brain at the last possible second.

"Sorry." She topped it off with what she hoped was a sheepish grin. "I guess I've been living in Santa Barbara too long."

"They call them *cows* in Santa Barbara? Remind me never to go there."

With pleasure.

Katie and Nicole edged their horses away, their blond heads bent together, skittering surreptitious glances in Moira's direction every few seconds.

"Now what're they up to?" she asked, still hoping to distract Dutch.

He shrugged. "Probably trying to figure out how sometimes you sound more like a dude than a dude."

ONE THING DUTCH LOVED about dude ranching was that it gave him plenty of quality time with Katie and Nicole. Where else could a man go to work and take his girls with him? Where else could they actually take part and help? On an eight-year-old level, of course.

"You two've been whispering up a storm ever since we headed out."

They glanced at each other as if they'd actually thought no one had noticed.

"What's up?"

"Can you keep a secret—"

"—Daddy? A really big one?"

He gave the question the serious consideration they expected. "I reckon I can."

"We're pretending Chloe is a princess—"

He didn't mean to grin; he couldn't help it. "I think she'd kinda like that." He wouldn't like it, of course, but he'd lived with Nicole long enough to know that sometimes that's what little girls grew up dreaming about.

"—an' she traded places with a look-alike and ran away to this country."

"I see I'm gonna have to quit reading fairy tales to you two."

"But, Daddy, they look so much—"

"—alike."

He'd noticed it, too. "Lots of people look alike. Doesn't mean they swapped places with each other."

"But they could."

"Besides," he continued, "she'd have an accent."

"She talks different than—"

"—us."

"I mean she'd have a European accent. You heard some of those interviews on the TV special. She'd talk like that."

They cast doubtful looks between them.

"And she'd be all prissy and snooty."

"Why?"

"Because royal people're different, that's why. They have hundreds of people to do stuff for them, so they're used to giving orders right and left."

"Chloe can be pretty—"

"—bossy sometimes."

It warmed his heart to have a discussion like this with his girls. At eight, they were like little adults sometimes; they could carry on real conversations, albeit with slightly warped logic.

"She's supposed to be bossy in your lessons. Besides, if she were a princess, she sure as heck wouldn't take a job on a dude ranch. She'd have a bank full of money and live in a mansion with lots of servants.''

"Maybe she's always dreamed of—"

"—living on a ranch."

"Then she'd buy one and own it. She wouldn't show up with a battered suitcase and move into our dormitory. She wouldn't know how to do everyday things that we don't even think about."

"Like what?"

"I don't know."

"Like drive a—"

"—Jeep?"

He shrugged. "Yeah, like that."

"Or how to cook—"

"—our cook says she's useless in the kitchen."

"Lots of people can't cook." He didn't sound very convincing even to himself. No need to tell them Chloe couldn't even operate a can of whipped cream. No sense adding fuel to their fire.

"Or like tightening my girth?"

"Now, she said she'd been stung by a bee."

"Uh-huh."

"Besides, I'm talking about other stuff. She just wouldn't be like a normal person, and Chloe seems pretty normal to me. So quit pretending."

"But why?" they wailed together in a tone designed, he was sure, to make him think he'd gone too far. He might be relatively new at parenting, but he wasn't stupid.

"Because I know you two. You'll get carried away, and the next step'll be thinking she's related to you somehow, and then you'll start believin' it."

"But..."

He chuckled. "And a princess sure as hell—sorry,

heck—wouldn't be caught dead on a dirty, dusty cattle drive without a feather mattress in sight."

"WHY ARE WE STOPPING HERE?" Moira asked Katie late that afternoon.

Katie twisted onto her stomach and slid to the ground in one smooth motion. "Daddy likes to overnight here."

"But there aren't any cabins," Moira said without thinking.

"Of course not."

Tents. She should have known.

"We sleep under the stars on a cattle drive. Didn't you do that where you grew up in Texas?"

On the ground? "Oh. Uh, yeah. I just thought...the guests would expect better accommodations, that's all."

"If this was Texas, where would you put your sleeping bag?" Nicole asked.

Was this a trick question? "On the ground."

They rolled their eyes. "Where would you wash up?"

Moira had watched enough movies to handle these two. "In the river."

"Upstream—"

"—or down?"

"On the shore." *Was it called a shore?* As much as she'd had to sidestep all their princess/castle questions in the past week, she'd rather have those than these. Familiar traps were better than the unknown. "You two've been here before. Why all the questions?"

"We bet a princess never—"

"—went camping."

Whoa! Did they suspect something after watching that darned TV special?

She took a deep breath, dismounted slowly and took a moment to loosen the girth a tad, giving them time to forget they'd even made such a comment. "Guess I'd better go help the cook."

"You don't have to. Daddy—"

"—hired a new man."

"Really?" Her pleasure was short-lived. "Not that paparazzo, I hope."

"Is that a European—"

"—word?"

"Sounds like it, doesn't it?"

"Where'd you learn it?"

"My girlfriend's studying in Europe, Miss Nosy." She cupped her hand by her ear. "Did you hear that?"

"What?"

"Your dad called you," she lied. "And don't ask *him* so many questions. You'll drive him nuts."

"It's time to get our sleeping bags—"

"—an' we're gonna collect firewood an'—"

"I'll be along later."

She hoped they'd soon realize they'd had a full day and were too tired to keep talking about princesses. *European word, indeed.* Where'd a pair of eight-year-olds get an idea like that?

If they didn't quit on their own, she'd have to find a way to distract them before someone else overheard and got suspicious. Like the paparazzo, if that's who the cook's new helper was. Dutch hadn't minded the guy dropping by the dining hall during lunch. It'd be just like him to invite the guy along for "some really good pictures." She couldn't risk her face gracing any page of any paper again. If he was on the drive, she was going to have to keep her distance from Dutch.

And that was a truly depressing thought. That meant the next time he cued his horse to shoulder in on hers, she'd have to side-pass right on away from him. Far enough that a camera lens couldn't catch the two of them together.

Too far for her.

"GIT IT WHILE IT'S HOT!" the cook hollered at sunset.

Moira was in no hurry. She sat on a log and studied the new helper as guests and wranglers alike lined up at the plank counter set up ten feet behind the chuckwagon. He wasn't paparazzo—at least not the one she'd "met" so far. If he was trying to blend in with the wranglers, he wasn't doing a very good job. While they were friendly and outgoing with the guests, he wore his hat brim low and ducked his head. Their shirts and jeans were soft with months of wear; his ill fitting. They laughed and joked and teased; he either nodded or shook his head in short jerks.

He doled out food the same way. *Whoosh. Slap.* A quick jerk of his head meant *move on!*

A long, strong leg stepped over the log. "Not hungry?" Dutch asked as he hunkered down beside her.

"Mmm, starving."

He clapped his hand on her knee. "Well, then, let's get some grub."

Who wanted to go eat when she could have his hand on her knee? It was warm, strong and oh, so masculine. "I thought I'd let the guests go first."

"They're all in line. C'mon." He held out his hand as he rose.

She debated whether she wanted to get anywhere

near the new guy. He was so...different, he could be paparazzo, but she supposed he had his hands too full ladling out food to wield a camera. Slipping her fingers into the warm comfort of Dutch's grasp, she rose and walked beside him to the end of the line.

The three clean-cut, college-age wranglers bringing up the rear immediately stepped aside. "Go on ahead, boss," Tim said in a respectful, yet friendly, manner.

"Thanks, but we're fine."

Out of nowhere, Ben brought up the rear, and Moira wished she and Dutch had taken the wranglers up on their offer. She still didn't know what to make of Ben following her all the time.

The line moved quickly under the efficient and experienced guidance of the cook. Before she knew it, Moira was next. The new helper barely peeked out from under his beat-up brim at her, reached beneath the plank and fumbled around.

"Does this bring back memories of Texas?" Dutch asked.

She knew if she hadn't had her hat on, his breath would have teased her hair near her ear as if it had on other occasions when he'd gotten close to speak to her. But she wasn't about to take it off before she knew if that fumbling idiot was going for a camera. If so, she was ready to bean him.

He apologized in a mumble, then ladled her up a heaping portion of stew that nearly overflowed the plate. He plopped on a biscuit and held it out to her, never meeting her eyes.

It was Katie and Nicole's fault for making her so cautious, so suspicious, with all their questions.

"Thanks." She accepted her plate, grabbed a can of lemonade out of the tub of ice and headed for a spot on one of the many long logs scattered in a loose circle around a small campfire.

She was glad when Dutch chose to sit next to her. She hadn't seen much of him all day. Every time someone had started singing a song, she'd found a reason to take off before he discovered she didn't know it. Except for the few she'd come across years ago in her music studies, like "Down in the Valley."

"Look at the sunset, girls," Dutch said softly. "Isn't it beautiful?"

Obediently they looked and nodded.

Dutch elbowed Moira. "Bet you wish this drive lasted more than two nights."

Guess again. "Oh, yeah. Sure do. Is this stew spicy, or is it just me?"

Dutch grunted in appreciation of his rapidly disappearing portion. "Must be you. I'm going back for seconds. Can I bring you anything?"

"More lemonade."

"Girls?"

Katie and Nicole, sitting on the ground in front of her, shook their heads and continued to pick the peas out of their stew.

"Hey, you eat those," he ordered with a crooked grin. He watched as they each ate a third of the stash they'd gathered in a napkin. The other third went into Nicole's shirt pocket after he was out of sight.

Just as Moira finished her lemonade, Katie and Nicole giggled.

"What?"

"If you keep drinking like that, you'll be—"

"—peeing in the woods all night."

Her throat closed up so fast, she was lucky she

didn't spit lemonade all over her lap. *The woods? I have to pee in the woods?*

At night?

IN THE MOONLIGHT, with millions of stars twinkling overhead, Katie and Nicole stood in front of Moira with their rolled up sleeping bags hugged to their chests. "We want to sleep by you."

Moira, her assigned sleeping bag tucked beneath her arm, stared long and hard at the ground. Somewhere, hidden in all that trampled down green stuff, lived slimy, leggy creatures, she was certain. Creatures that bit or buzzed or crawled or itched. Maybe all four at once. Whatever they did, she didn't want to meet them.

And now it seemed she had witnesses, too. "Won't you have more fun with the other kids?"

They grinned and shook their heads, sending their long braids flying so much that Moira nearly didn't notice their pixieish expressions. They were up to something, and they weren't saying what.

Dutch strolled over and dropped his sleeping bag. It landed with a plop near the toes of her boots. "Here, I brought you a flashlight." The glow from the campfire emphasized the twinkle in his eyes, making it sparkle and jump. "I know you're gonna need it."

She accepted the flashlight gracefully, knowing she needed it already.

He perused the ground and kicked aside a couple of small rocks. "This looks like a good spot." He graced Moira with a devilish grin that would get him just about anything he wanted. "You don't mind sharing, do you?"

"Mmm, no." He'd done his best to bump knees with her on horseback, to fondle her shoulder in the chow line, to touch her leg during supper. She could only wonder what he had planned for lying beside her, each of them in their own zippered-up bags, with two dozen chaperons nearby.

"Good." He hunkered down, untied his sleeping bag and rolled it out.

Moira watched with interest, determined to learn quickly, though her gaze centered more on the play of his muscles beneath the broad expanse of his chambray shirt than on what his hands were doing. There was just enough moonlight to admire him all she wanted, but not so much as to make her preoccupation obvious.

"You gonna stand there all night?" he asked.

"I thought I might help the girls."

As he looked over at Katie and Nicole, she followed his gaze. They'd unrolled their sleeping bags so close they were practically on top of each other.

"They're old hands at this."

"So I see."

"Kind of like you were at their age, I imagine."

She dropped her bag, waved the flashlight self-consciously and said, "I'll be back in a few minutes."

Her trip into the woods was hesitant, to put it mildly. She wasn't sure how far to go to guarantee the privacy she needed, so she kept on walking, thinking she always saw a darker spot just ahead. A dormitory bathroom suddenly didn't seem so bad as it had on her first day. At least it had individual stalls with flush toilets and clean seats.

At this point, any seat would have been nice.

The glow of the campfire lit her way back to the

campsite, where she slipped out of her loose boots, made a mental note to buy a new pair that fit as soon as she got her next paycheck and crawled into her sleeping bag.

She squirmed this way and that, trying to find a comfortable spot.

Dutch's soft snore clued her in to the fact that yes, it was possible to sleep on the cold, hard ground.

She wiggled her behind to the left of one rock, her shoulders to the right of another.

"Whatsa matter—"

"—can't you sleep?"

"I can't find a good spot."

Katie and Nicole giggled.

"What's so funny?"

"Isn't it soft enough—"

"—for you?"

"Not hardly. Feels like every rock in Colorado's under me."

The giggling was replaced by a flurry of whispers.

"If you two can read each other's minds, how come you have to whisper?"

"'Night, *Chloe*."

"Yeah, 'night, *Chloe*."

By the time she woke up needing a second trip into the woods, everyone seemed to be asleep. She didn't go quite so far, but kept imagining she heard someone following her with a similar need. She didn't want to get stumbled over while she had her jeans bunched around her knees, so she sang softly.

A bare glow from the embers in the firepit lit her way back.

The first pink streaks of dawn painted the Eastern sky when she woke up with the urge to make her third trip into the woods. "Woke up" was using an expression which didn't quite ring true, given the fits she'd suffered over the rocks.

It was way too cold to crawl out of her toasty sleeping bag, except that she knew if she waited, she'd have to go farther into the woods to be alone. So far, only the cook and his helper were up, poking around behind the chuckwagon with breakfast preparations. Not even the birds were up yet, but their chirps were imminent.

Katie and Nicole slept with their heads ducked into their bags. Just lumps under the slick blue covers.

Dutch, on the other hand, didn't seem to notice the temperature, if his arm thrown across her body was any indication. He didn't even have a jacket over his shirtsleeve to keep warm. Her dry lips cracked with a small smile as she watched him sleep. Sprawled on his stomach, his dark hair rumpled, his cheek dark with beard stubble—she drew on all her movie-watching experience and tried to picture him in the same bed with her.

She'd never shared a bed with anyone, so she didn't know what it would feel like to have someone so near. She had to be content with what it would look like. Dark hair on a white satin pillow slip. Down comforter pulled up but not quite covering a broad, bare shoulder. His long legs tunneled under the covers.

She inched her leg closer to his, then came up short against the margin of her sleeping bag. She glanced around, saw no one was watching and kicked her bag closer to his. Her leg hit his with a thump. Instead of waking, he snuggled closer. She pressed against him, finding solid muscle and bone. He murmured in his sleep and bent his knee.

She burned to unzip both their sleeping bags and get closer. No one would notice. No one would see.

One of the wranglers yawned and stretched, punched his buddy next to him and started to rise. If she didn't head for the woods right away, she was going to have company. Lots of it.

It was just barely light enough to leave the flashlight behind. Light enough now to see her warm breath fog up the cold air like a puff of smoke. As other wranglers rose, she hiked farther away than she had during the night. When she found a dry creek bed, she followed it for easier going. From the sounds of the herd stirring, she was headed in their direction, which meant more wranglers, so she backtracked and took the creek the other way.

A sharp crack in the distance sounded as if someone had stepped on a dry branch. She began to sing softly, as she had the evening before, so no one would stumble across her, until she realized she couldn't even hear herself for all the noise.

Thunder?

Men shouted, cattle bellowed, hooves pounded. If she didn't know better, she was hearing—

No, it couldn't be. This wasn't a TV Western. She tugged her jeans up and zipped them in record time. TV Western or not, there was a stampede brewing.

Toward her? Or toward Katie and Nicole?

And Dutch, zipped up in his sleeping bag like a trussed-up turkey.

Chapter Ten

Dutch tugged his arm into his sleeping bag, then wondered why the heck his fingers were numb. He hadn't felt cold all night. Hot, as a matter of fact, sleeping next to Chloe. Just using the words "sleep" and "Chloe" in the same sentence were enough to heat his blood to an uncomfortable degree.

And it wasn't sleeping he'd be doing with her.

He grinned to himself and wiggled in her direction. When he didn't bump into her, he scooted closer. Finally he had to open his eyes to see why he could smell the lilacs that followed her everywhere, but couldn't make contact.

She was gone. Again. Her scent lingered, teasing him until he pulled her sleeping bag over and wadded it into a pillow. He inhaled deeply, savoring her scent, though it was nothing compared to the real her. Was she up for the day or just making another trip to the woods? He closed his eyes and hoped she'd come back and curl up next to him to get warm.

Get real. Chloe wasn't that outgoing. Passionate, yes—he'd discovered that each time he'd kissed her. But to make a move on him on her own, he'd have to be dreaming. Since he was raising two impressionable children and since he'd hated the way Hollywood starlets had thrown themselves at him, he guessed he ought to be grateful.

But it was darned hard when he'd spent the entire night dreaming of just the two of them alone in his bedroom, serenaded by night sounds drifting in through the window he always left open.

He'd nearly turned his musings into a delightful dream when he realized he wasn't hearing any ordinary night/early-morning sounds. As a matter of fact...

Cattle bellowed.

The ground shook.

His eyes flew open. In a flash, he oriented himself, abandoned his bed to scoop up Katie and Nicole—sleeping bags and all—and stuffed them behind the nearest boulder.

"Stay here!" he ordered.

"What? Huh?" Katie and Nicole murmured.

To everyone else, he yelled, "Everybody up! Now!"

"Daddy, what's—"

"—going on?"

"Stampede. Stay there! Do you understand?"

Wide-eyed, they nodded. He would have preferred to see them duck down instead of peeking around the boulder, but he had to move around the campsite and warn the others.

"Up! Now! We got a stampede!"

The big teddy bear chuckled. "Nice going, Cordwin. Very effective."

His wife, as wide-eyed as the twins, reached over and shook him with both hands. "Honey, I think he's serious."

"Wranglers, move it! Get mounted!" He needed to put someone in charge of getting all the dudes to safety while he took charge of the herd. "Chloe," he bellowed, then remembered she'd been gone a while.

His gaze darted around the campsite and landed on the cook, who nodded and immediately took charge of the guests. "I saw her go into the woods, boss."

The sunrise was lost on Dutch, except that it had turned light enough for him to see her emerge from the woods at a run. Kind of a clumsy one, as if her boots kept sticking in mud, but he knew there wasn't any. She was halfway between the trees and the campsite when the first steers surged around the perimeter.

"In the creek," he murmured aloud, as if she could read his mind. "Get down in the creek."

For a gal from Texas, she didn't show much sense. Barefoot, without time to think about what he was doing, he set out to do what he could. He ran toward her. The ground shook beneath his soles as the cattle picked up speed. The thundering noise drowned out his calls to her.

Couldn't she see the dry creek bed beside her?

In a flying tackle, he hit her broadside and took her over the edge with him. Suspended in air, he wondered if it had been a smart move. Unfortunately it had been his only choice. Together, they landed in a heap on a bed of gravel with her on the bottom. Air whooshed out of her lungs.

Without pause to assess any damage, he deftly rolled them both back toward the four-foot high bank. A dozen feet flew overhead. Scores more followed. He pulled Chloe beneath his body, covering her, protecting her as dirt and rocks poured down on them, as tons of beef thundered over them. Without his hat to protect him, debris pelted his hair and rolled past his collar, filling his shirt with half of Colorado.

She coughed beneath him, and he pulled her closer until her nose was buried in his chest. His was immersed in her hair, but the lilacs had been overpowered by the stench that was uniquely cattle. At least she was unhurt.

Well, if his flying tackle hadn't busted any of her ribs, she was.

In the meantime, for long moments after the cattle had passed, he got to crouch out of sight of everyone else and hold her wrapped tightly in his arms. To feel her chest rise and fall with each attempt to breathe through the dust. To feel her heart pound beneath him. To feel too damned much when there wasn't anything he could do about it at the moment.

"You okay?" he asked.

Her head bobbed against his chest.

"Nothing broken?"

"I...don't think—" she coughed up dust "—so."

"Everything's okay, then?"

"Yeah—" she coughed again "—you?"

As soon as he was convinced she was all right, the way she'd taken a foolish chance with her life made him mad. "Why the hell didn't you jump into the creek?"

"I had to—" cough "—get back to the girls."

Her head shot up, swiveled in the direction of the campsite. He was surprised by her answer, but not so surprised that he didn't shove her back down as a couple of stragglers hurdled the bank.

"You were going back for Katie and Nicole?"

She pushed against his chest. "I've got to go see—"

"They're okay." If there were more women in the world like her, he hadn't been lucky enough to run across them. He held her firmly, determined to hang on to her as long as he could. "They're fine," he said soothingly. "I dumped them behind a boulder where they'd be safe."

He brushed her hair off her face, letting his palm linger on her cheek to reassure and comfort her, letting himself touch her, hold her as long as possible before people started running their way to see if they'd made it.

"Besides, I don't think the herd went through the camp."

As the dust began to settle, he peered over the edge of the bank for any more crazed cattle. In the distance, the wranglers who'd been able to get on horseback were doing a heck of a job circling the herd and bringing it under control.

And who was out in front? None other than Ben.

"Looks like MaryAnne was right about him."

Chloe followed his gaze. "Is that Ben?"

"Yep."

They rose side by side and watched him ride his cow pony as if they'd been glued together.

"Dang, I want a raise." She laughed. Dutch knew it was at the absurdity of thinking she'd taught the man everything he knew.

"MaryAnne said he was cowboy through and through. I didn't believe her." Frustrated that he'd been fooled, he shook his head, when what he wanted to do was shake some truth out of Ben. "But nobody gets that good that fast. Come on, I'll help you climb out of here."

He let her go up the bank first. Not because he was

a gentleman so much as because that way he got to place his hand on a very nice derriere and give her a boost. And she didn't seem to mind. She even reached down and gave him a steadying hand when it was his turn.

She brushed dirt out of her hair, running her fingers through it and making blond waves go every which way. "So why the subterfuge?"

"Guess that's what I'll have to find out." That is, if he could keep his mind on business instead of on watching her brush off her shirt and jeans. Though just thinking about the possibility of her lying trampled beneath the cattle was enough to send him into a rage.

"Good luck. He's pretty good at covering up."

Dutch flexed his fists. "Oh, he'll talk."

Now that Dutch had some money and a measure of fame, was someone out to get him? Someone who had risked the lives of Chloe, Katie, Nicole, MaryAnne, and all the others? Had Ben started the stampede then covered up his part in it by coming to the rescue?

"Let's go see what the hell he knows."

He stopped short when her hand landed on his arm, transferring a sense of urgency from her to him. She peered down, then bent at the waist for a closer look at his feet.

"Ohmigod, is that blood?"

"Didn't have time for boots." He glanced down at his toes, then zeroed in on her sock feet. "What's *your* excuse?"

She glanced back toward the woods. "I guess they fell off."

"*Fell* off? Darlin', I use a bootjack at night. How the hell could yours fall off?"

She frowned at his lacerated feet. "You shouldn't walk on those. Let me go get you a horse."

"Chloe..." he warned.

She sighed, then met his gaze with a steady look. "They're a little big, okay?"

It didn't take a flash of genius for him to realize what she didn't want to say. "Chloe, wearing hand-me-downs isn't something to be ashamed of."

Her eyes widened like a doe in headlights.

"Lots of people find themselves short of money. It's not a crime."

Her shoulders softened and she seemed to relax. "Yeah, I guess."

He slung his arm around her, smiled to relieve her embarrassment and glanced meaningfully at the dry creek. "Can you believe those fools in Hollywood told me I couldn't do stunts?"

She laughed lightly and tilted her head up to him. "No."

Determined not to miss any more opportunities, he dipped his head and claimed her lips in a kiss that he'd intended to be gentle. After the harrowing experience they'd just been through, it was anything but. Mirroring the passion of the chase, the thrill of the capture, the impact of their tumble, his mouth opened on hers, tasted her darkest, sweetest recesses and ignored all calls to come up for air.

To think it could all have ended so differently. That he might never have kissed her again. Might never have held her in his arms again. Might never have gotten to make love to her and show her how much he could care for a woman who'd risk her life for his children.

She was pliant against him, her bones softening so that they were nearly as one. As close as they could be right then; not nearly close enough.

When she dragged her lips from his, he tucked her head beneath his chin. Their heartbeats slowed together, allowing them both time to compose themselves.

In the distance, the camp pulled itself back together on one side, the wranglers calmed the herd on the other. As much as he wanted to walk off into the sunset with her, it was only the beginning of a brand-new day. And he had something important to do. Something that couldn't wait for her to go get him a horse.

"Come on. Let's go get some answers."

WHEN BEN RETURNED to the campsite, MaryAnne jogged over to him before he had a chance to dismount. Her hand landed on his thigh as she gazed up at him with concerned eyes.

Dutch watched as the cowboy dismounted, then allowed himself to get pinned between the horse and MaryAnne, allowed her hands to touch his arms, his cheek, his chest.

"Would you look at that?" Dutch muttered from his seat on a log. His legs stretched out in front of him, Chloe was bandaging his right foot, the cook his left. "Somebody get me my boots."

Katie and Nicole, who had looked entirely too serious when they'd seen the cuts on his feet, ran and got them. "Here, Daddy."

"Thanks, girls." He pulled his socks out of them and tugged his foot out of Chloe's hands.

With both hands, she grabbed his jeans over his calf and hung on like a terrier. "Oh, no, you don't. You're not putting dirty socks back on over these bandages."

"We'll get you some clean socks—"

"—Daddy." They ran off.

In the meantime, he got his toes cradled in the valley between her breasts, which was almost enough to make him forget about Ben. Until he saw MaryAnne stretch up on her tiptoes and kiss the cowboy's grizzled cheek. Apparently she was letting her feelings get in the way of her better judgment.

"What the hell's going on?" Dutch muttered.

"Looks like she decided he's okay," Chloe said with a dismissive shrug of her shoulders.

Dutch snatched his socks from Katie and Nicole as soon as they ran back, rammed his feet into them, then into his boots. Aware that his stride looked more like Marshall Dillon's gimpy deputy than the macho image he preferred, he hobbled across the campsite, clapped one hand on Ben's shoulder and spun him around. "What the hell do you think you're doing?"

"Hey!" MaryAnne said, and tried to brush him off.

With the back of his arm, Dutch wedged her away from Ben. "This is between us. Now, Ben—if that *is* your real name—I want some answers, and I want them now."

MaryAnne squeezed herself between the two men and faced off with her brother. "Cut it out, Dutch."

Grasping both her arms, he firmly set her aside. "Go on over there by Chloe while Ben and I get some things straight."

"You have no right!"

Ben interjected with a calm drawl, "Now, MaryAnne, it'll be all right."

She gazed up at him. "You have no idea how pig-headed my brother can be."

"Damn straight." Dutch knew Katie and Nicole were listening. He didn't care. There were times when a man had to be a man and say things that had to be said. "For starters, tell me who the hell you really are, 'cause it's a sure bet you aren't some dude."

MaryAnne fisted her hands on her hips. "You don't have to tell him anything."

Dutch glared at her. "You're the one who told me to keep an eye on him. Whose side are you on, anyway?"

"That was before I checked him out."

"Before you—?" Dutch scratched at the stubble covering his jaw and tried to figure out if she was speaking in code. "How the heck did you do that?"

She glanced around at the curious crowd Dutch's theatrics had drawn, and lowered her voice so just the three of them were privy to the information. "He's got an excellent reputation down in Houston. He was on the police force there."

Ben's stony glare softened into a grin. "You checked me out?"

Dutch suddenly felt as if he were in the middle of a Ping-Pong tournament, as Ben and MaryAnne focused in on their own little world and ignored him.

She shrugged. "Sorry. I had to."

"How'd you do that?"

"I hired someone."

His grin spread across his face. "Well, I'll be danged."

"Yeah, me, too," Dutch said shortly. "What else did you find out?" His sister paid him no mind, so he got in Ben's face. "What the hell are you doing here on my ranch?"

"Told ya. I'm resting up from a leg injury."

"Bullsh—"

"Daddy!"

Dutch wrapped his fists in the front of Ben's shirt. "Talk fast, cowboy, or you an' me are gonna take a walk in the woods."

"For heaven's sake, Ben, if you're following somebody, tell him," MaryAnne pleaded cautiously.

Ben remained silent.

"Fine," Dutch snapped. "We'll go in the woods."

"Okay by me."

He shoved Ben in front of him as they walked away from the crowd of guests and wranglers.

"Hey, man, you did a great job turning the herd," the teddy bear said.

Others chimed in. "Yeah, thanks."

"Don't know what would've happened without you."

"You learned to ride like that in a week and a half?"

As Dutch heard them, he remembered that Ben, in spite of being on the ranch under false pretenses, had been the deciding factor between safety and possible disaster.

"Okay," he said when they were out of earshot. "Just give it to me straight."

Ben glanced around, seeming to weigh his options. "I've been hired to follow someone."

"Someone here?"

"Yep."

"You're sure? You've already found him?"

Ben nodded. "I'm sure."

"And what's supposed to happen next? You tell someone he's here? You take him away? They come get him? What?"

"I'm just supposed to follow someone. Nothin' else. I don't even tell anyone where we are."

Dutch was sure he must've hit his head in the creek. "That doesn't make sense. People have other people followed in order to make them disappear."

Ben laughed, a full, rich sound. "You watch too many movies."

With his hand shoved against Ben's chest, Dutch sent him reeling backward. "This is my ranch. These are my guests. I want you outta here."

Ben shook his head. "They'll just send someone else. Look at it this way, my cover's blown. I'm a known quantity now."

"Then you're no good here anyway."

"Sure I am."

"How's that?"

"Simple. The person I'm following hasn't a clue about being followed."

Dutch gave it a moment's thought. His guests left every week or two. "When he's gone, you're gone?"

Ben nodded. "Then I'm outta here."

"And what about my sister?"

"Well, hell, I didn't say I wouldn't be back."

AFTER BREAKFAST, Dutch addressed the guests. "We can continue the cattle drive as planned, or, if y'all prefer, we can get you back to the ranch."

"You mean quit?"

"You mean skip the cookout tonight?"

"You mean we wouldn't sleep under the stars again?"

"No way!"

Dutch grinned at the wranglers. "Sounds pretty unanimous to me." He smiled at the guests. "Mount up!"

Moira was never so glad to get her bare feet off the ground. Katie and Nicole had searched for her boots and returned with trampled leather, no heels in sight. Everyone had packed only what fit in their saddlebags. There were no spare shoes to be had.

"Can you ride like that?" Dutch asked. "There's always the chuckwagon."

She didn't want to be restricted to any wagon unless he was with her. "Where will you be?"

"On my horse."

She adjusted her hat and wiggled her toes in the stirrups. "Me, too. I get a breeze this way."

He shrugged with a good-natured smile. "Whatever turns you on."

"'Sides, we want to talk to Chloe, and we can't all fit—"

"—in the wagon."

As Dutch took off his hat and eased his big bay closer, Moira held her mare still. When he was as close as he could get, he hooked one hand around her neck, leaned over and kissed her. Right in front of everyone.

She felt her cheeks blaze. He kissed her there, too, then grinned that devilish grin of his that made her burn all the way down to her toes.

"I've got work to do. You girls go easy on her now, hear?"

"Sure—"

"—Daddy."

Moira, Katie, and Nicole rode silently side by side after Dutch cantered away. Katie and Nicole stared at her until she looked at them, then they glanced quickly away. They kept on like that for fifteen minutes, after which time Moira thought they should have gotten tired of their game.

"What's up with you two?"

"How'd you sleep—"

"—last night?"

"You mean when I wasn't peeing in the woods?"

They giggled. "Did you feel—"

"—anything?"

"Nah, I took the flashlight with me and didn't go in too far."

"Not that! Did you feel—"

"—anything?"

"Like what?"

"Anything!"

"Sure."

They both gasped and looked at each other as if they'd just discovered a hidden treasure. "What did you feel?"

"Cold air," she snapped. "My sleeping bag." Then it dawned on her, and she grinned. "Oh, I get it. Yeah, I felt something."

"What?"

"As if you didn't know."

"What?"

She was too smug at figuring them out to be shy. "You saw your dad sleeping with his arm around me, didn't you?"

"Not that," they wailed together. "Under you."

That wasn't what they meant? "Under me? You mean, like rocks? Yeah, I felt them, all right."

"There weren't any rocks—"

"—under your sleeping bag."

"Yeah, there were."

"Nuh-uh. We kicked 'em—"

"—away. Before you turned in."

"Well, you missed some."

"All you had under your sleeping bag were some peas—"

"—that we put there."

"Peas? You mean the ones you didn't eat at dinner? Why would you do that?"

If she could have interpreted the looks they gave each other, she might have understood.

"You mean you don't—"

"—know?"

"Girls, I haven't a clue what you're talking about."

"You never heard the story 'bout the—"

"Never mind!" Nicole screeched at her sister.

LATE IN THE AFTERNOON, they camped alongside an upper section of river that afforded good wading—if one didn't mind the temperature slightly above frigid. Katie and Nicole couldn't have cared less.

"Can we go swimming now—"

"—Daddy? Huh? Please? Huh?"

"I can't come in with you girls, so you'll have to stay where it's shallow."

Dutch watched their little heads swivel right on over to Chloe, just as naturally as if she'd been part of their lives for months, not a week and a half. "Will you come in with us?"

"I think I'll stay on shore and keep your dad company."

Katie opened her mouth and started to speak. Nicole jabbed her in the ribs. "Okay. See ya."

Dutch felt...warm inside. Yeah, that was the best way to describe it. Warm. Chloe might not be openly demonstrative in front of others for, oh, another hundred years or so, but this was a step in the right direction. At least she'd admitted out loud that she wanted to spend some time with him.

He sat on rocks worn smooth by thousands of years of river flow, and patted a spot beside him. Then he kept his eyes firmly on Katie and Nicole, and let Chloe take her time sitting beside him.

She pulled her knees up near her chest and wrapped her arms around them. "How're your feet?"

"Let's just say I was real glad to be riding today."

"Yeah, me, too. I've got on three pairs of socks, but they're not very cushy."

Ever so gently, he leaned sideways until his shoulder brushed hers. "Did I thank you?"

"For what?"

"Running back to save my girls?"

She laughed. "Yeah."

"What's so funny?"

"Well, it kind of got lost in the 'What the hell were you doing?' roar that went with it."

He chuckled along with her. "Sorry about that. I was upset." The understatement of the year.

"Mmm."

They watched the sunset together in silence, though he was really keeping one eye on the twins and the other on the play of shadows on Chloe's face. When the cook announced supper, they made sure the girls

were out, then hobbled through the chow line together.

"Sloppy joes. Yummy. Where's the—"

"—peas?"

Dutch couldn't believe what he was hearing.
"Okay, who are you and what did you do with Katie
and Nicole?"

Their shrugs were innocent enough, but their grins
had a long way to go if they wanted to convince anyone.

The cook frowned at Chloe. "What happened to
your boots?"

"Stampede."

He turned to his helper. "Hey, Luiz, give her your
mitts."

"My mittens?" Luiz asked with a heavy accent.

Dutch spoke right up. "Hey, whoa. She's not
working tonight."

"Nah, these'll make good slippers." He reached
over and grabbed them off Luiz's fingers, which sent
the helper into a flustered rush to wrap towels around
his hands. "Fool kid must have hands of wax if he
can't touch them spoons without padding. Here, slip
'em on, sweetheart."

Dutch took one look at her feet in bright orange
mitts with the thumbs sticking out to the sides, and
bit his tongue to keep from laughing. She looked like
a bird. True, the cutest, biggest one he'd ever seen,
but a bird, nonetheless.

Katie and Nicole broke up laughing.

"Now, girls, that's not nice," he said, barely able
to keep a snicker out of his voice.

"Go on, laugh if you want," Chloe said to all three
of them. "At least I can walk now."

"Good, then you can fetch my guitar for me later."

Supper was quiet that night, which it always was the second night out. Between the long days, hot sun and fresh air, everyone was well relaxed. Tomorrow they headed home.

"I'll take that guitar now," Dutch hinted to Chloe.

"Why?"

"Whaddya mean 'why?' So I can play it while we sing, of course."

"I don't know. Everyone looks mighty tired."

A general murmur went around that convinced Dutch they all wanted their evening sing-along. Reluctantly, it seemed, Chloe fetched his guitar from the chuckwagon.

"Let me play it for you," she offered when she returned.

From the way she clutched it to her chest, he thought he might have to wrestle her for it. A delightful thought; well worth considering. "Why?"

She shrugged. "I'd like to help. And your feet are sore."

"I don't play with my feet."

She mumbled. Katie and Nicole shrieked with laughter.

Dutch narrowed his gaze with suspicion. "What did you say?"

"Nothing," she said with an innocent air.

"She said it sounds like you play it—"

"—with your feet."

He looked up at her. "You think you can do better?"

"Mmm-hmm."

"This, from a lady who wears orange oven mitts on her feet?"

"Yeah, well, at least I admit they look funny."

"Oh, so I play funny?"

"Oh, heck, Dutch, she's a music major," Dave said. "She probably thinks we all sing funny, too. Let 'er play."

"A music major? I don't remember that on your résumé."

She sat next to him, strummed the strings, then set about tightening them.

"What're you doing?" He grabbed for the guitar.

She twisted until it was out of his reach unless he crawled over her. Another thought worth considering.

"Tuning it."

"It's in tune."

"Maybe for a coyote."

When she strummed it again, he grudgingly admitted—to himself—that it sounded better. "Do you know Clementine?"

"Just start. I'll manage."

When he got to the part about Clementine's shoes, he improvised a loud and hearty "oven mi-its, with the thu-umbs, sticking ou-ut, for Chlo-oe."

She laughed as hard as anyone, and, for the first time, Dutch lost his place in a song. He'd meant it to be a joke, picking that song, but it turned out to have sadder lyrics than he'd ever noticed before. He didn't want to think about losing her—he'd come too close just that morning. He certainly didn't want to sing about losing her.

And when the end of the summer came, he didn't want her to go.

He didn't know how to ask her to stay without scaring the devil out of her. She'd gotten riled when he'd suggested she move into his lodge. No telling what she'd do if he proposed anything else.

IF MOIRA THOUGHT she'd been tired the first week she'd worked on the ranch, it was nothing compared to that night. But no matter how much she wanted to drift off to sleep, it didn't happen with Katie and Nicole, snug in their sleeping bags, giggling and whispering beneath the star-studded sky.

She groaned and rolled over, but they didn't take the hint.

"Hey, girls, knock it off," Dutch ordered. Quietly, for Moira's ears only, he murmured, "You awake?"

"I'm too cold to sleep."

His answering chuckle was deep and low, and made her think he was up to something.

"I can fix that."

She heard the zipper on his sleeping bag, then hers. She imagined everyone in Colorado heard them and knew he was up to something.

Warm arms scooped her up and dragged her in with him, then pulled her bag over on top of them.

"Better?"

When she nodded, her cheek rubbed against his soft chambray shirt, the top of her head beneath his hard chin. "Well, I'm warm."

"Good. Go to sleep."

Like this? Stretched out chest-to-chest, with her half on top of him, his heart beating steadily beneath hers?

I'll never be ready for this.

"You never told me what you found out about Ben."

"Ah, it's nothing." His chest rose and fell beneath

her, like a wave beneath a boat. "He's just trailing somebody. He'll be gone soon."

The only person she'd seen Ben trailing was her. And MaryAnne, of course. But as far as Moira knew, no one knew where she was to follow her. When she'd visited Ennsway for the king's funeral, she'd shown Chloe the brochure from the dude ranch, but Chloe wouldn't have had her followed.

"Who's he after?"

She felt his shrug, and she snuggled closer. If Ben wasn't gone soon, should she find a way to get rid of him? Just in case? She hadn't any money to bribe him. No muscle to threaten him.

The steady beat of Dutch's heart beneath her was hypnotic. Her eyelids grew heavy. Her breathing relaxed. As soon as she set her worry over Ben aside, she remembered what the twins had said earlier.

"Dutch?"

It was a moment before he murmured, "Hmm?"

"Why would the girls put their vegetables under my sleeping bag?"

"Mmm."

That was all she got out of him. Even Katie and Nicole had settled down. The camp was quiet. She drifted off.

Dutch mumbled a few words, then added a clear, "Love you."

Her eyes flew open. She forgot her next breath. Wanting to make closer contact with him, she finger-walked up his chest and neck, over his stubbled chin until she felt his lips, cool from the night air. She turned his head toward hers and whispered, "What?"

He opened his lips. And he snored.

"Dutch?"

Another snore.

Had she heard him correctly? Was he talking to Katie and Nicole? Or to her?

Or had she been dreaming?

DEEP IN THE SHADOWS, a man hunkered down beside a broad tree trunk. His gaze was focused on one sleeping bag only, and the two people in it.

Everything had worked out beautifully. Well, almost everything. He fit in well on the ranch and cattle drive. No one suspected he had started the stampede. Unfortunately, as with his other plans to do her in, he had been unsuccessful. She *would* pay, though.

Idly, he rubbed the scar on the back of his hand as he thought long and hard about another way to end her life. It would not do to make it quick. He owed her so much more.

Somehow, someway, he would use what was important to her. He would use it against her. He would take it the same way she had taken what had been his.

She was too close to Dutch and his brats. She did not deserve to be happy.

Chapter Eleven

For the first time in more years than she could remember, Moira dreamed of her mother. Queen Alexis, every bit as exotic as her name, had died of a lingering illness shortly after Moira turned ten.

Why am I dreaming of her now?

As the sun rose over the mountain crest and warmed Moira's face, the only parts of her body she dared move were her eyelids. This moment was too precious to let go, too rare not to want to understand what had prompted it.

Beneath her head and the half of her body sprawled on him, Dutch's chest rose and fell in a slow, relaxing rhythm. Beneath her ear, his heart beat steadily. She listened carefully, feeling it was trying to tell her something. To remind her. To show her the way.

Once she thought about it, she supposed she'd only heard one other person's heartbeat in her life: her mother's. Vaguely she felt the long forgotten comfort of nurturing arms around her, heard the soft voice that used to sing her to sleep or laugh with her over some silly thing that amused them both.

No one had even attempted to replace her mother. If they had, she probably wouldn't have let them, but, all the same, no one had even tried. At ten, she could have used a woman's warm touch, a soft smile, an avid listener. A bit of loving guidance through her teen years wouldn't have been shunned. Emma had been the most wonderful personal secretary, but that's all she'd been.

Beneath her, Dutch began to stir.

Just a little longer. Just until I can remember what she looked like.

While Alexis's features were dimmed, the clear hazel eyes were the same ones Moira saw in the mirror every morning. So, she still had something of her mother after all.

Warm hands stroked her back; big, masculine hands capable of playing with two little girls without breaking them. Capable of making her feel warm and cozy and loved.

Loved? Startled by the thought, she popped up onto her elbows, one of which landed in Dutch's ribs and startled him awake.

A slow smile spread across his face, lighting it as the sunrise did the land. "'Mornin'," he drawled.

"'Mornin'."

Awareness of his erection prodding her thigh, where she had it oh-so-casually draped across him, made her wonder how he could sound so natural when he was experiencing something so...monumental. At least for her it was. If a man had ever had such a reaction to her before, she hadn't been aware of it.

A couple of her past escorts—very carefully selected escorts—had obliged her with a perfunctory kiss at the end of an evening out. Whether their reticence had something to do with her status or was due to the bodyguard's glares, she wasn't certain. It really didn't matter. She'd tried to encourage the ones she'd liked with soft smiles and whispered words, but had gained no satisfaction to her curiosity.

She supposed if she'd really liked any of them well enough, she'd have found a way. But she hadn't.

Until now.

"Do you remember what we were talking about last night?" she asked. She not only wanted him to remember, but she also wanted him to say it again. It was the only way she would know for sure what he'd said, to whom he'd been referring.

He blinked, as if it was too early to remember much of anything, and his devilishly sexy grin showed he was comfortable with his guilt. "Nope. Can't remember anything till I've had my coffee. You mind gettin' your elbow out of my gut?"

She scooted away.

"Wrong way, darlin'." He dragged her back and settled her on top of him.

Full-length, thigh-to-thigh, she'd never even danced so close. She lowered her head onto his shoulder and closed her eyes. She rose and fell with him like a boat moored safely within its harbor.

"What were we talking about?" he prompted. "Last night."

She shrugged. "I'm not sure. I...I guess I'd just dozed off when I heard you say something. But I'm not sure what it was."

"Well, if it was important, I'll say it again."

Would he? If she stuck to him like glue all day? She wasn't even sure he'd been talking to her, so it could be an exercise in futility.

When she opened her eyes again, Katie and Nicole

were staring at her; their blue eyes open wide, windows to their curious, mischievous natures.

"'Morning, girls," she said, so Dutch would know they were awake.

He turned his head toward them. "'Mornin', munchkins. Sleep all right?"

They giggled. "Yeah, Daddy, we slept fine. Was Chloe's spot uncomfortable—"

"—again?"

His arms snuggled her tighter. "She was cold."

"Daddy, if you marry a princess, would that make you a prince—"

"—or a king?"

"I have no idea."

"I bet Chloe knows, don'tcha—"

"—Chloe?"

Moira pulled the sleeping bag over her head and wished the call of nature to overtake the two of them.

"Still cold?" Dutch rubbed her back briskly.

No sooner had she opened her mouth to answer than she had two little girls launch themselves onto her back. Dutch must have seen them coming because, instead of having the air whoosh out of him, he chuckled deep and low, the sound echoing from his body right into hers.

She felt like sandwich filling. No, she corrected, the center of a cookie, surrounded by hardness and sweetness and temptation.

A metal spoon clattering against a skillet put an end to the moment. "Come 'n git it!"

MOIRA STUCK TO DUTCH all day. Where he rode, she followed, even if it was just behind brush to pick up a straggler. Where he sat for lunch, she joined him on a large, flat rock, though she knew, in front of the others, he'd never say what she wanted to hear.

That afternoon, they returned the cattle to their home base. When the horses were all handed over to the wranglers and the shadows started lengthening, he directed Katie and Nicole toward the first van.

"Chloe, you take the other one."

Hope fell as he followed them to their ride. He'd go back with them. They'd have supper in the Saloon where she'd be expected to mingle with the guests, not leech herself to him. What had she been thinking? He was probably glad to be rid of her.

She climbed into the van. The teddy bear cupped his hand on her shoulder as he stooped past her to a seat farther back. "Great time, wasn't it?"

"Mmm," she murmured absently. Great time, if one didn't mind diving into rocky creek beds or freezing her butt off at night.

Nancy plopped onto the seat beside Moira. "Can't say I'm in any hurry to get back to the kids, but I won't miss that hard ground."

Neither would she, though technically she'd only spent one night on it, since last night she'd spent practically on top of Dutch. And it had meant nothing to him, apparently. She blinked back tears and stared out the window so no one would notice she missed him already.

"Hey, Nancy—"

Like a drowning woman, Moira quickly swiveled toward Dutch's baritone. He leaned in the doorway, the sun behind him, his arms spread wide with a hand on either side of the frame.

"—you mind letting me sit there?"

Nancy laughed and shouldered Moira, then whispered, "Go get 'im, girl," as she got up and moved.

Moira turned back to the window and swiped away her tears.

"You okay?"

She nodded. "Just got something in my eye."

"Let me look."

"It's okay now." Slowly, hoping her eyes were drying up by the millisecond, she turned to him.

His gaze was steady, unsuspecting. "Must've washed it out."

"Yeah." She smiled. "Whatever it was."

"How 'bout singing something, Dutch?" Dave asked. "Like—" Whatever he'd been about to say was cut off with a bark of pain. "What? What'd I say?"

Moira suspected his wife Nancy had a hand—or an elbow—in stopping him, but others picked up the impetus and called out suggested songs.

"Well," Dutch drawled, "I don't have my guitar with me."

"That's okay," the teddy bear said. "Now that we've heard Chloe play, you're better off without it."

"So what you're saying is, I'd better not count on a career as a singing cowboy?"

"Oh, you can sing all right," Dave admitted. "Just not with a guitar in your hands."

Dutch tilted his head and peeked at Moira from beneath his brim. "Sounds like something you'd say."

She struggled to look innocent, batting her damp eyelashes until his serious facade broke into a grin.

"Okay, then." He slung his arm around her shoulders and started them all off on a sing-along.

Moira didn't know the words, but hummed along as she picked up the melody.

Dutch's breath was hot on her ear. "What are you doing tonight?"

She forgot to hum, but peeked sideways at him. "Why?"

He shrugged. "No reason."

"Oh." She shrugged, too, lifting his arm with her shoulders. "I was hoping you were asking me out for an ice-cream sundae, but..." She stretched that last "but" out a long, long way.

He sang with the rest of the group for a moment before he answered, soft and low. "I have ice cream up at my place."

"Is that a bribe?"

He grinned mischievously. "Hey, whatever it takes."

"So, let me get this straight. You're asking me up to your place for ice cream with you and the girls?"

"Nope. The girls are spending the night with MaryAnne."

"Oh."

"You're gonna make me ask, aren't you?"

"If you've got something to ask."

He nodded. "I do." He sang along some more, picking up the guests' flagging pace, making her wait for his low, intimate invitation. "Will you come back with me tonight?"

All day she'd stuck to him, wanting him to talk to her. All day, he'd been Mr. Sociable with his guests. Now he wanted to be alone with her.

And she didn't think it was talking he intended on doing.

"Yes," she said. When his arm tightened around

her, she knew, in her heart, that was the right answer. Even if she *was* the wrong woman.

THEY RETURNED to the dude ranch none too soon for Dutch. Unfortunately it was time for a chili supper. While he should be thinking of a hot bowl of chili, he was, instead, anticipating a hot night with a woman he really cared about.

He'd startled himself just as much as her when he'd said he'd loved her last night. He knew she'd heard him; she'd nearly jumped out of his arms. In fact, it was her reaction that had startled him to his senses.

He'd never told a woman he'd loved her. Why last night? He hadn't even made love to her yet. How could he know?

As everyone piled out of the two vans, Katie and Nicole ran to Chloe and hung on her, jabbering about something or other. She smiled down at them, laughed with them, gave a hand over to each of them to be dragged into the Saloon.

How could I not know?

MaryAnne fell into step beside him. "Chloe sure is good with Katie and Nicole."

"Sure is."

"I know they need a mother, but I hope you aren't stringing her along for their sakes."

"Stringing her—? Dammit, MaryAnne, I'm not the stringin' type."

She laughed. "Oh, yeah, Mr. Blunt-and-to-the-point. What was I thinking?"

"I have no idea." He held the door for her.

"That's why you tried to sweet-talk me into taking Katie and Nicole for the night."

"Sweet-talk?" He grinned. "Darlin', that's just me."

"Yeah, well—" she ground her index finger into his arm "—just be careful who you turn all that charm on, mister. I like Chloe, and I don't want to see her or the girls get hurt."

"Yes, boss," he teased.

"I mean it, Dutch."

"I know you do. 'Scuse me, okay? I want to be sure to get a seat next to Chloe."

As popular as she'd become with everyone, he thought he might have to wrestle a chair right out from under someone, but he found the one next to her still empty. Around the table were the teddy bear and his wife, Dave and Nancy, and Larry.

Dutch shook the latter's hand before he sat down. "Hey, everybody, I'd like you to meet my agent, Larry. Larry, this is—"

Larry waved him off. "We already introduced ourselves."

"So what brings you all the way out here to—what did you call it? Mount Forsaken? Rattlesnake Ranch?"

Larry's smile was rueful. "Did I mention how pretty it is out here?"

"No."

"'Course, I wouldn't want to hide myself out here, you understand. Not with all those beautiful, unattached, Hollywood women waiting for me."

"Uh-huh."

"You, too, Dutch."

He peeked at Chloe toying with her chili, stirring her spoon around in the bowl as if she'd lost interest. After a long day in the fresh air, that wasn't possible.

Everyone else was starving; he could tell by the way they shoveled it down.

He didn't want her to get the wrong idea about women and Hollywood. "No one's waiting for me there, Larry."

Larry cuffed Dutch on the arm. "Oh sure, man, they are. I guar-an-tee it. Matter of fact—" he reached into his breast pocket and withdrew a folded sheaf of papers "—I have here an offer that'll prove it to you. Remember that script you liked?" He tossed the papers onto the table in front of Dutch and smiled broadly at everyone else. "They want you to do it."

"Really?"

"Yep. With the hottest female lead in Hollywood."

"Julia?" Dave and the teddy bear asked at the same time.

Larry puffed up. "Would I get anyone else to star opposite Dutch Cordwin?"

A collective murmur of consent circled the table, stopping just short, Dutch noticed, of Chloe.

"You sign this, Dutch," Larry continued as he tapped his finger on the pages, "and I'll guar-an-tee you more publicity than ever."

"More paparazzi?"

Larry waved his hand again, as if trying to erase that image, then shrugged and laughed. "Well, of course, we can't ever get rid of them. But I'm talking respectable journalism now, buddy. Legitimate interviews. Family photo sessions in your lodge."

Chloe's chair scraped the floor as she stood abruptly. Automatically Dutch reached out and touched her arm. First she didn't eat much. Now she was done? She must be more tired than he'd thought.

"You ready to go?" he asked.

"Nice to meetcha," Larry said in dismissal. "Now, Dutch..."

Dutch rose beside Chloe, stayed close, spoke softly. "Tired?"

"Yeah, I guess."

"If you want to rest a spell, I can come by your room and pick you up when I get done here."

"Sure."

He didn't think she sounded too sure, but she graced him with a soft smile, so he let her go. For what he had in mind later, a little rest now wouldn't be out of order.

Larry tapped his finger on the papers again when Dutch took his seat. "Look here, Dutch. Have you ever seen that many zeroes behind a number?"

Dutch tilted his head for a closer look. His eyebrows lifted in acknowledgment. "Can't say as I have."

Larry laughed as if he'd just sealed the deal. Which he had, because Dutch knew if he took this offer, buying Chloe a trained trick horse would be the least of the gifts he could shower on her.

DUTCH PUSHED OPEN the always-unlocked front door of his lodge, letting it swing inward as he politely waited for Moira to precede him inside. She did so with trepidation.

Oh, she wasn't afraid of him. She wasn't afraid of being alone with him. She wasn't afraid of what she knew he had planned.

Well, maybe a little. But she trusted him.

What scared her the most was that things had gotten this far, that she'd fallen in love and hadn't been honest with him.

Should she tell him she wasn't really Chloe Marshall? Well, why? Because it would be honest, for one thing; something Dutch put great store in. Because she didn't want to spend the rest of her life looking over her shoulder, waiting for the sky to fall. But most of all, because she loved him.

She turned to face him. "Dutch..." She walked right into the circle of his arms, touched her lips to his and forgot everything she'd just figured out.

His lips were dry from the sun, his arms strong from ranch work, his chest hard against her breasts because he was a man, and she a woman. And she knew she was about to discover for herself all that entailed.

"Chloe."

That brought her to her senses again—for all of a second. She couldn't help herself. She'd never felt this way. Never experienced such desire. Never had a man's hands roam her body like Dutch's were doing, plunging through her hair one minute, cupping her derriere the next. He pulled her close, ground himself against her so there was no mistake in what she felt.

"Finally," he murmured against her ear. "I've wanted to be alone with you for so many days now. Chloe, you don't know—"

She wedged her hands between their chests and pushed. It didn't seem to have much effect.

"What?"

"I...we need to talk about..."

His lips blazed a trail through her hair. His tongue moistened the tip of her ear, then continued on its path.

"What? Oh!" He sounded as if he'd just figured something out. "Don't worry about it."

Don't worry about...what? "Dutch."

"I'll take care of it."

"Hmm?"

"It's okay. I understand."

"You do?"

She didn't, not anymore.

I'm not ready for this.

She knew her shirt buttons were open; she could feel the cool air on her skin, the rough calluses on his fingers, the heat from his palm as it cupped her breast. The moan she heard was hers.

The hell I'm not! Other than the creak of his spacious bed as they landed on it, the soft words Dutch whispered in her ear were the last sounds that she could put words to.

For a big man, he was so tender as he touched and stroked every inch of her body, branding her as his. He traced the scar on her inner thigh. Embarrassed at her imperfection, she pushed his hand away.

Gently his lips barely brushing her skin, he asked, "What's this?"

"Dog bite."

His chuckle was deep and low, and reassuring in its familiarity.

"Figures. You do crazy stunts on horses, and it's a dog that gets you."

She wondered if other couples talked in bed, but not for long. Where his hands went, his kisses followed, until she was lost in time and space, and needed no one but him. Always him. Always beside her.

For a rugged cowboy, he spoke mighty gentle

words—lover's words—which heated her body and melted her soul. Words she couldn't hear over the roar in her head, couldn't remember because they meant nothing compared to his touch. Always his touch.

It was worth more than her crown. It was worth her life to be loved by a man like Dutch. To be loved *by* Dutch.

She wanted to make his heart race as he did hers. Make him moan, too. Growing bold, she let her hands slip down his body, to explore him as he had her.

He sucked in a short breath, and she grew bolder.

She followed with her lips, as he'd taught her. Tried to put into her kisses all she'd received, even though she knew that wasn't possible. He hadn't spent his life deprived of touch, as she had. But she was sure no one had ever loved him as much as she did, and she tried to make it show.

Only it was so difficult to keep her mind focused on pleasing him when he slipped deep inside her. Impossible. She'd make it up to him later, when she could reason again. When she came back down to Earth. Which might be never.

WHEN DUTCH OPENED HIS EYES again, the first streaks of dawn had lit their way across his bedroom wall, turning it from white to pastel shades of pink and purple. Chloe was sitting on the window seat, her bare legs tucked up to her chest—which she'd demurely covered with one of his chambray shirts—and her arms circling them. Her chin rested on her knees as she stared outside.

He couldn't blame her. The view from his window took in the whole tree-filled valley below, some ridges and bluffs across the way. It seemed he always had a breeze there, and it ruffled through her hair, lifting the ends of it, making it tease her nose until she had to tuck the strands behind her ears.

"Come back to bed, darlin'."

She turned her face toward him, rested her cheek on her knees for a moment before she spoke. "We need to talk."

He hoped his grin was devilish enough to charm her back to his side first.

Her answering smile was soft and sad.

"Something wrong?" How could anything be wrong? He'd just woke up from the greatest sex he'd ever had. Even he knew it hadn't been just sex. He patted the mattress. "Come on. We'll talk in bed."

She went back on point with her chin on her knees. He sighed, threw off the sheet and padded across the hardwood floor to the window seat. If she saw how much he wanted her this morning, he was sure they'd be warming that mattress again in no time.

"Sit—" her voice broke "—down."

"Here? Oh, I get it. You like variety. Hey, I like variety, too." He sat on the cushion and got a throw pillow tossed onto his lap. He waggled his eyebrows at her. "Not quite what I hand in mind, darlin'."

She chuckled. "So I see. But the pillow'll have to stay there until I can say some things I need to say."

He studied her closely, could see that this was something important to her. Something she needed to get out of the way. He could wait, but only a little while. "Okay. Shoot."

"First—"

"First? There's more than one thing?"

Her sigh was one of exasperation.

"Okay." He settled his back against the wall and stretched one long leg out on either side of her hips. "But it won't be easy. I can give you, oh, maybe five minutes."

"Dutch—"

"Ten, tops."

She tipped her head in acquiescence. "Then I guess I'd better get to the point. First, are you going to do that movie?"

"Yep." He grinned proudly. Such a lot of money. "Signed the contract last night before Larry left."

"I see. And you'll be going away to Hollywood?"

"Oh, I get it." He was relieved, to say the least. He scooted closer and rested his hand gently on her shoulder to reassure her. He traced a circle with his fingertip. "Don't worry about it. I already made sure you and the girls can go on location with me."

She took a deep breath. "We'll come back to that one later. If you want."

"Not if it means I have to wait to drag you back to that bed and show you how much I lo—"

"But second..." She interrupted what he considered a crucial moment between most men and women. "Second, I want to talk to you about Katie and Nicole."

He took his hand back, contenting himself instead with studying how the rising sun highlighted her hair, how the waves were tousled from a night of lovemaking, of sleeping wrapped in each other's arms. "What about them?"

"You know how you hate it when they tease you?"

"Nah."

"When they trade places?"

"Oh, yeah. Well, swappin' places with each other's not good. It's not honest."

"Like people who pretend to be other people aren't honest?"

"Yeah, but why are we talking about them when we could be—"

"We're talking about me, Dutch."

"You?"

"Yes, me. I'm not who you think I am."

A chuckle welled up from deep within him. "Darlin', I *know* who you are. After last night, I don't think we have many secrets." Well, that wasn't true. He still had one.

She nibbled her lower lip with perfect teeth, then turned a gaze on him that worried the hell out of him. He'd never seen her look like that; loving and fearful at the same time, watery-eyed, like a woman on her way to the gallows.

"I'm not Chloe Marshall."

He started to object, then realized that, although his mouth was open, nothing was getting said. So he took a deep breath and tried again. "What do you mean, you're not Chloe Marshall? You mean you changed your name? Dammit, you're not married, are you?"

She looked completely taken aback by that question. "N-no," she stammered.

He breathed a sigh of relief. "Good. Now that you've scared me out of twenty years, tell me what the hell you're trying to say. Straight out."

"I already did. I'm not Chloe Marshall."

He mulled it over, the whole conversation, until the lightbulb inside flickered on. "You didn't!"

She nodded.

"You swapped places with Chloe?"

She nodded again.

He laughed.

"You're not mad?"

He slapped his thigh. "Well, I guess that's a good one on me."

"We didn't do it to tease you or trick you or anything. It wasn't personal. I hadn't even met you when we switched. Hadn't even applied for this job."

He thought she looked more relaxed now that she knew he wasn't going to toss her out the window. "So who are you really?"

"Oh, I can't tell you that."

The light at the end of the tunnel dimmed. "What?"

"I can't tell you."

"I *heard* you. I just couldn't believe it."

"It wouldn't be fair."

"To who? Me? Her? My kids? Who, Chloe? Or whatever the hell your name is." He rose from the window seat, shot the pillow across the room and yanked on a pair of jeans. No one could expect a man to argue without his pants on. "Tell me, 'cause I sure can't figure it out."

"To Chloe. She's made a life for herself. I can't jeopardize it."

"By telling me?"

"By telling anyone. I told you what's important, Dutch. I've been honest with you. I wanted to tell you last night before we made love, but..." Her words trailed off.

"But what?"

She shrugged. "I couldn't."

"Couldn't? Or wouldn't?"

"I...I've never felt that way before. I couldn't think. I couldn't speak."

He shook his head. "Yeah, I noticed. And I thought you were just too embarrassed to ask me to use a condom."

She ducked her head. "That, too."

Whoever she was, she could be brave and passionate one minute, shy and demure the next.

"I was going to tell you I love you."

"I know," she said softly. She peeked at him from beneath her lashes. She didn't ask the obvious question. "I wanted to stop you so you wouldn't have to take the words back later. If you wanted to."

He rubbed the back of his neck, which hurt like holy hell this morning. "I don't know what I want. Get dressed. We're going back to the ranch."

Chapter Twelve

Sunday was arrival and departure day for many of the guests. Moira stood in the center of the laundry room, housed in the old-time Barber Shop at one corner of the town square. A cool breeze blew in through the door, chasing out some of the heat generated by six noisy, industrial-size washers and dryers.

Today was also the day that the real Chloe, in her letter, had arranged to pick Friday up at the airport. Moira wouldn't miss the dog. Those low, rumbling growls used to scare her. Now they just made her nervous.

"You can use those machines over there," Gina told her as she left with a mountain of neatly folded sheets.

Over to the right, Moira found two smaller machines for the employees' personal use. That was her, all right—employee. Though she didn't know for how much longer. She supposed it depended on how mad Dutch got when he found out there was no way she was going to divulge her real identity. Eventually he'd probably get tired of waiting and fire her.

In two weeks, she'd fallen in love, then completely sabotaged the relationship. Frustrated with how quickly she'd fallen for a man, how she'd failed to make a successful, happy life for herself as an average American woman, she shook her head.

"Need some help?"

She spun around to find that Ben had entered the laundry room under cover of all the humming, sloshing machines.

"I saw you shake your head," he said with an understanding grin. "I thought you might need someone to decipher those buttons for you."

"Really?" she said airily. "It's not like I've never done this before."

"Oh, yeah. Guess you're right."

She glanced around. They were alone; maybe Ben would confide in her. "Dutch says you're following someone."

He tugged his hat down a notch. He studied the toes of his dusty boots. "I 'spect a person gets some funny notions out there in Hollywood."

"Mmm." She mulled over his noncommittal reply. "So what are you doing in here?"

He held up a stuffed pillowcase. "I was gonna do wash, but—" he indicated her two sacks with a nod of his head "—it looks like you got both machines covered."

She'd gotten the idea to use pillowcases from watching the girls in the dorm. Now she wished she'd tagged along to see how laundry was done, so she could start hers in front of Ben, just like any other woman could do.

"Yeah," she agreed, wishing he'd leave her alone to figure this out. She upended a bag into each machine, spilling tank tops and lingerie over the sides and onto the concrete floor. Her cheeks hot with embarrassment, she scooped the clothes up before everyone on the ranch knew she was partial to bright, lacy bras and panties.

"You're s'posed to sort stuff," Ben said.

She whirled on him. "You're following *me*, aren't you?"

His frown appeared genuine. Like a true gentleman, he kept his eyes above the delicates clutched in her grasp.

"Now why in tarnation would I do a thing like that?"

"That's what I'd like to know. You were following me the night I went into the office. You show up at every riding lesson, but you need lessons about as much as I do. You were one of the few wranglers up at the time of the stampede."

Suddenly, hearing the words out loud, she realized what that could possibly mean. Dutch had told her he'd never seen a stampede before, and hc didn't know what had caused the one they'd watched from the creek. Had Ben started it? Was that even possible?

She must have looked frightened, because Ben stepped forward and laid a gentle hand on her shoulder before she had the presence of mind to scoot away. Unfortunately her retreat was blocked by the machine at her back.

"Hey, I'm no threat to you," he said.

"Then why are you following me?"

He glanced around. He studied her carefully, as if weighing his options. He nodded, as if having a conversation with himself. Then he said, quite clearly, "Emma sent me."

The room swam. Her knees buckled.

"No." Her denial was barely audible, even if she'd

been in a quiet room. With her back to the washer, she slid down. She landed on her derriere on the concrete floor with a thud. "Emma?" she whispered weakly.

Ben crouched in front of her. "You all right?"

"Why would she do that?" It was a rhetorical question. "She practically raised me. She knows how important this is to me. To do this on my own."

"She thought you might need a little protection."

She clapped her hands over her ears for a brief moment. "No!" She scrambled to her feet, and he followed. "This is exactly what I don't need."

"You aren't supposed to know."

Her laughter was short and none too sweet. "I'll bet. You pack your bags and get off this ranch."

He scratched his chin, behind his ear, his chest where his shirt V'd open, obviously stalling. "Well, I could do that…"

"Today."

"But if I do, she'll just send someone else. Wouldn't it be better to pretend you don't know?"

"I'll go where she can't find me." It was an empty threat. She knew she wouldn't leave unless Dutch fired her, but Ben didn't know that.

He shook his head apologetically. "I wouldn't let you out of my sight that long."

She turned back to the washers, frantic for the knowledge that would show her how to get them going so she could get out of there. It was so important for her to do these things for herself. It was so important to be average for once in her life. It was just so damned important…and in danger of being stolen from her.

All she saw were buttons and dials. Frustrated, she

kicked the machine. She randomly pushed and turned anything on the back panel that moved. She stuffed her scraps of lingerie in with everything else, slammed the lids shut as if she were trying to shut out her past and shoved past Ben.

"We'll see about that," she challenged.

DUTCH HAD JUST SPENT the worst twenty-four hours of his life, and he wasn't even sure how he'd spent them. Was he angry? He hadn't a clue. Puzzled? Still no clue. His feelings were all jumbled up, had him strung tighter than a bale of straw.

MaryAnne had accused him again this morning of being grouchier than a bear with a sore paw. Katie and Nicole elected to spend their time elsewhere. They'd been with him up until two hours ago, when he'd stared into the laundry room and seen Chloe— or whoever she was—turn her back on Ben and kick the machine.

Departing guests were the only ones who didn't have the sense to stay out of his way. Dave clapped him on the shoulder. "Hey, Dutch, helluva week."

Dutch grunted an indecipherable reply. *What had she and Ben been talking about?*

"Yeah, too bad we didn't get pictures of the stampede," Nancy added with a big smile. "The kids're so jealous." She threw her arms around his neck and hugged him goodbye.

His arms circled her automatically; he was that kind of guy. But he noticed she didn't feel like Chloe. This woman's breasts mounded against his chest didn't push any of his buttons. He knew it didn't have a damned thing to do with her husband standing right there.

"We'll be back next year."

Was Ben following Chloe? If so, then he knew who she was.

Dutch snapped his fingers, sure that he had a clue he could work with. All he had to do was find Ben and get some answers out of him. Any way he could.

"Well?" Dave asked.

"Huh?"

"Nancy asked if Chloe would still be here next year."

"Hell if I know."

"Well, uh, we're going now."

"Huh?"

"Van's waiting."

"Oh, yeah." Dutch pulled himself together long enough to shake the man's hand. Business was business, after all. He wanted his guests to leave happy and come back again. 'Course, if the stampede hadn't scared them off, he doubted his surly mood would. "Have a nice flight."

Dave, Nancy, and their kids walked across the town square and, along with others, boarded the first of two vans departing for the airport. Chloe, sporting a tie-dyed tank top, met them at the side door. There was another piece of the puzzle; no clue about sorting clothes before she washed them. From the way it hugged her breasts, it looked as if she'd shrunk it, too. She got in with them, talking and laughing as if they were going on a picnic instead of parting.

There'd been other clues, too. The cook said Chloe hadn't a speck of skill in the kitchen; couldn't even boil water. Dutch was reasonably sure now that she hadn't stepped in any hole the night of the square dance; she probably didn't know how to dance, either. Trouble with Katie's saddle?

Nah, that one didn't count. How could anyone who knew so much about horses not know how to adjust a saddle? What else?

Ah, yes, the whipped cream episode. It was obvious she'd never handled a can of whipped cream before. Where was she from? Mars?

When her dog jumped in, the door closed, and the van pulled out, Dutch realized something was amiss. Sure, he could see her riding along to the airport to bid friends goodbye, but not taking her unsociable dog with her, too.

He wanted to pretend it didn't matter. He wanted to say "good riddance" and toss her personnel file into a fire. He wanted to forget MaryAnne had found him three different trick horses from which to choose a gift for Chloe. But he couldn't.

Well, he'd have to forget that last one. Whoever she was, she probably didn't know beans about trick riding, either.

His suspicions about her leaving were confirmed when Ben ran down the row of cabins, got into his own car and lit out after her.

Dutch's chest constricted. He didn't want her to leave this way, without saying goodbye, without kissing him again, without giving him a chance to get over being deceived.

Would I get over it?

Maybe. Being on the lam from some killer would be a pretty good reason for going into hiding. But not for keeping her identity a secret from the man she loved.

Does she love me? He thought she did.

In spite of not knowing for certain who she was, he knew he loved her too much to let her leave this way. He had to tell her.

Galvanized into action, he stormed over to the driver of the second van. "Get out."

"Wha—?"

He yanked the door open and bellowed, "Get out!" When the wrangler was slow to move, Dutch grabbed his shirt and gave him a helping hand into the dust. He slid behind the wheel and hollered, "Buckle up!" to everyone in back.

WHEN DUTCH LOST SIGHT of the first van in the city an hour later, he knew it was fortunate that he at least knew where it was headed. Of course, if Chloe jumped out anywhere along the way, he'd lose her. But what better way to run away than hopping a plane? He screeched the van to a halt in the designated shuttle area and leapt out.

"Hey, Dutch—"

He heard one of the guests start to ask him something. He simply ignored it as he charged into the terminal.

At the gates, he scanned the crowd, cursing a blue streak because Chloe was too short to stand out. Even if she did, her straw cowboy hat would blend in with so many others.

And then he saw Ben, a good head taller than most, heading away from him. He followed him to a noncommercial area, to a secluded gate. Beyond him, he could see Chloe and her dog walking side by side. A security guard approached them, but, once he saw Friday's lip curl, he backed off and got on his radio instead.

A hundred feet to go, Dutch strode past a wide pillar. That was all the farther he got, as Ben stepped out and flattened a hand against Dutch's chest.

"This is as far as you go, Dutch."

"Get the hell out of my way."

Ben shook his head. "Can't."

"And I can't let her go." He made a fist.

"Look, she's not—" Ben's words were cut short by a punch to the jaw. His knees crumpled, and he sagged to the floor.

Dutch had the presence of mind to drag the fallen cowboy behind the pillar, lean him back and tilt his hat forward as if he were taking a nap. It only took a few seconds. Then he looked around for Chloe again. He didn't see her or the dog. He scanned the area quickly.

Outside, a black-and-white blur caught his eye as it raced across the tarmac. Friday headed straight for a private jet, ran up the steps, launched herself on someone standing in the doorway, and disappeared. A moment later, he saw a hand reach out and wave, and then the door closed.

Had Chloe already gotten on the plane? He scanned the outside of it for identifying numbers, for anything he could possibly use to trace it. All he saw was a flag decal, and one that seemed familiar. Where had he seen that before?

When he remembered, he couldn't believe it. The TV special he'd taped for Katie and Nicole. The wedding of the century between the king of one European monarchy and the queen of another. Their two flags had been combined into one for the new country of... Something or other that started with a *B* was all he could remember. He hadn't really paid much attention; it didn't concern him.

Not at the time anyway. Now seemed to be a different matter entirely.

But wait! If someone in the plane had waved, that meant Chloe was still on the ground, didn't it? But which Chloe would it be? *They look alike.*

They know each other.

She thinks it's cute when the twins swap places.

Nobody had to draw him a picture except maybe to tell him *which* Chloe was on the ground now. The real one, or the princess?

He glanced around. He ran from one end of the area to the other. He went to get Ben and shake some answers out of him, but he was gone, too.

"Damn!"

WHEN THE VAN DROPPED HER off back at the ranch, Moira was both intensely sad and unreasonably happy at the same time. She'd gotten no more than a glimpse of Chloe, her best friend, but it had been enough to see her radiant smile. Moira didn't think it was solely for the reunion with Friday. Chloe was happy and content in her new life.

Moira could do nothing to jeopardize that. After all, when she ended up happy—if that were possible after this two-week fiasco—she wouldn't want Chloe to let the truth escape. Truth that could pull them both into an international scandal, which would be the least of their problems. Moira remembered William, Chloe's new husband, as a headstrong boy. He'd surely grown into a strong-willed man who'd toss Chloe into his dungeon and throw away the key.

She'd ducked into the first shuttle van at the last

possible minute, knowing Ben was watching her, praying he'd follow her. Hopefully she'd lost him at the airport. Hopefully he'd think she either boarded a commuter plane and eluded him, or boarded Chloe's jet for a quick drop-off somewhere else in this country. Hopefully he'd be too disgraced to return to the ranch for his things, but would keep on moving.

In the meantime, she'd like to find Dutch and see what his mood was at the moment. See if he'd had enough time since yesterday morning to cool off.

"¡Señorita!"

Just about to enter the dorm to drop off her jacket, Moira was approached by a distraught-looking Luiz.

She grinned. "The cook find you useless, too?"

He shook his head. *"Señorita, las niñas…"* He frowned, looked like a man who wanted to tell her something important, but couldn't come up with the right translation fast enough.

She probably looked as confused as she was. Living in Santa Barbara had given her some basics in Spanish, but what girls? She'd never actually spoken Spanish to anyone, but she gave it a stab. *"¿Qué niñas?"*

"Katie y Nicole. Señorita, vámonos."

There was no mistaking the urgency in his voice and posture as he darted back and forth, urging her toward Dutch's Jeep.

"Slow down, Luiz. Tell me where they are."

"¡No, no! ¡Katie y Nicole! Vámonos."

Moira didn't know what was wrong, but she was determined to find out. She followed Luiz to the Jeep, wondering if the twins had gotten into some kind of trouble and were hiding from their father. Maybe they'd sent Luiz to get her, knowing she was more tolerant of their pranks than Dutch was.

She peered into the Jeep, hoping to see them hiding behind the seats, which she did. Their eyes were wide with fright. Red bandannas gagged their little mouths.

She spun on Luiz. "Back off."

"No. You get in," he ordered.

Surprise made her ask, "You speak English?"

"So it seems."

"Then why—?"

He shoved her onto the passenger seat. She tried to yell at him to stop, to attract attention, to turn around so she could kick at him. She had to overcome him so she could help Katie and Nicole.

He smacked her so hard her teeth rattled, her ears roared, her vision blurred.

"Shut up!" He spit in the dust.

He climbed over her, tramping on her carelessly as he did so, then slid behind the wheel and started the engine. As it roared to life, Moira worried about the two precious lives on the floor behind her. Whatever it took, she had to save them, had to see that they got free, that they were returned to Dutch unharmed.

Why had this madman picked them? What could he possibly want with her and the twins?

Why the hell did I ditch Ben at the airport?

As if knowing she needed an answer to her questions, her abductor tore off his glove and shoved the back of his hand six inches in front of her face. His scarred hand.

Prince Louis, her brother.

Chapter Thirteen

Moira's teeth rattled as Louis rocketed the Jeep up the mountain with her and the twins at his mercy. His driving skills were even more limited than hers; the Jeep swerved drunkenly along the narrow, winding strip of road, making Moira wonder whether they would reach the top or plunge hundreds of feet into the boulder-strewn valley.

"Slow down!"

"So you can jump out? I think not."

"I wouldn't leave the girls." It was the truth.

Katie and Nicole, in the back, remained silent. While Moira had the relative comfort of the padded seat—and had buckled her seat belt when her head finally cleared—the girls were stuck on the hard floor until Louis swerved to a stop in front of Dutch's lodge.

"Everybody out."

"Gladly!" If he'd left the key in the ignition, she'd have thrown it into the forest, but he pocketed it in his jeans.

She couldn't imagine why he'd brought her to Dutch's lodge, unless he'd been using this as some sort of hideaway and didn't know it was Dutch's. But rather than take the time to ask, she wanted to see how Katie and Nicole had fared.

She leaned between the seats and spoke in as normal a voice as she could muster. "Come on, girls. Let's get out before he decides to drive somewhere else." Katie wiggled to her knees, and Moira gathered her in her arms. "I'll get you in a second, Nicole." She turned and slid off the seat to the welcome stability of safe ground.

When Louis reached in to retrieve Nicole, Moira quickly untied Katie's hands and feet, putting her body between them so he couldn't see what she was up to.

She whispered, "When I tell you to, you run and don't stop. Not for anything. Okay?"

Katie nodded, though not as enthusiastically as Moira would have liked.

Louis shoved Moira. "Stop that."

As soon as he set Nicole down, Moira thrust her hands against his chest and shoved him back. "I will not, you little turd."

Katie reached for Nicole's bonds, and Moira concentrated on keeping Louis too busy to notice. She shoved him again, sending him back two more steps.

"What kind of creep are you, picking on defenseless little girls? What are you doing here?"

He laughed at her and turned toward Nicole, then Katie, and back again. "Moira, you should introduce me, no?"

"You won't be around that long."

His face sobered. "Katie, Nicole... Which is which, I wonder? I cannot tell the difference. No matter. I am Moira's brother, Louis."

He smiled at them, and Moira wanted to rip his face off.

From ten feet away, Katie and Nicole stared at her as if they couldn't believe their ears. "Moira?" Eyes wide with surprise and glee, they turned to each other and squealed, "We were right!" They hugged and hopped up and down, screeching loud enough to send bears racing for cover.

Louis took a reeling step backward—a good thing in Moira's estimation—so she let Katie and Nicole have their fun.

"You really are Princess—"

"—Moira! We knew it. We put the peas under your sleeping bag and we—"

"—knew it!"

"What are they jabbering about?" Louis asked.

"Got me."

"What does that mean?"

"What?"

"'Got me.' What does that mean? Why do you—"

He hadn't a chance to finish. Katie and Nicole, no longer fearful, pranced right up to him and stared in awe. "Are you a—"

"—prince? For real?"

He scowled at Moira. "I should have been a king, but for your interference."

She debated on arguing with him, on denying she was his sister, but after having received Chloe's letter, she knew it was useless. He'd tried to assassinate Chloe; it was a sure bet he wasn't here to celebrate Moira's new job.

Katie grabbed his hand. "Louis—"

He yanked it back. Moira looked on in pity, knowing Louis, too, had never received his allotment of friendly gestures, casual touches. He had so much to look forward to, if only he would take a chance.

"She won't bite you, Louis."

He folded his arms across his chest, tucking his hands safely beneath them.

"Louis—"

"Your Royal Highness, to you," he snapped at Nicole.

Katie and Nicole screeched with delight. "A prince! He's really a prince! Right here in our yard."

"Shut up!"

Holding hands, jumping up and down in circles, they tuned him out.

"Let them go," Moira said.

"What kind of fool do you take me for? I am not the little boy you knew in Ennsway."

She shrugged, and resisted the temptation to answer the question. "You don't need them. I'll do anything you want."

"I want you to call Dutch."

"Okay."

"I want him to bring me money."

She nodded. "I'll tell him whatever you want."

"Tell him to bring five hundred thousand dollars."

Moira felt her eyebrows arch into the treetops.

"This is not enough for you? I am afraid I am not very good with American currency yet."

She snorted. "It's enough for ten of me, you idiot."

"All the same, it is what I desire. You cheated me out of much more by taking away my crown."

"It wasn't yours."

"If you did not want it, you should have abdicated."

"It wasn't mine at the time, either, if you remember. Father was alive when I traded places with Chloe."

The twins screeched again.

"Stop that insufferable noise!" Louis yelled at them, shaking his finger at them as if it would make a difference.

Katie and Nicole jogged circles around him, looking him over from head to toe, making observations.

"I thought princes were taller—"

"—and darker—"

"—and handsomer. Where'd you get the scar—"

"—on your hand?"

He bent down, leveling his menacing glare with their curious faces. "I got it while trying to kill my sister when she was a noisy little brat like the two of you."

Moira stared at him. "What?"

He turned to her with a smile all the more evil because he didn't have to work to make it seem so.

"You did not know that, did you?" He meandered a couple steps nearer. "Yes, the 'accident' with the horse was supposed to hang your neck up in the rope, not my hand." He nodded, as if she needed confirmation. "And the dog I sicced on you, too. I do not know how you are so lucky, Moira."

She wasn't feeling too lucky at the moment.

"Well, your luck has run out. Running you off the road might not have broken your neck—"

"You didn't!"

He laughed. "Yes, Moira, I did. I also beat up the cook's assistant so I could get closer to you. Had I known you could elude a stampede, I would have poisoned your stew instead of spicing it. As it was, you made all those trips into the forest for nothing.''

He clapped his hands one time and smiled as if his luck—and hers—had changed.

''But no more. Now, I have—how do you say?— all aces. You will call Dutch and tell him my demands.''

Moira took a deep breath. ''Katie, Nicole.'' She waited for their attention. ''I want you to walk down the road now.''

''No,'' they wailed together.

''We want to ask the prince some—''

''—questions.''

''Now.''

''No, you do not have to walk away.'' Louis's voice rose to a thunderous roar as he continued, ''But you must stop going around and around me! Have you no respect?'' He yanked his hand away from Nicole, who'd managed to snatch it again.

''I'll make the call after they leave. Girls, start down the road now. Head for the ranch. You can find your way, can't you?''

''But, Chloe—''

''—Moira, we don't want to leave.''

''You have to.''

''No,'' Louis barked.

Moira tucked her hands into her front pockets. ''Then I won't call Dutch.''

''I will drive them back to the ranch after you do what I say.''

''Oh, yeah, right.''

''You do not trust me?''

''Not you. And not the way you drive, either.''

''Bah, the Jeep is no good.''

"It was fine when I drove it. You're a lousy driver, just like you were a lousy brother." Maybe insulting him wasn't the way to go. "You don't need them, Louis. They'll just ask a million questions and give you a headache."

He gazed down at them. "They are rather noisy. But how do I know you will make the call?"

"You have my word."

His laugh was short. "You must do better."

"If I don't call Dutch, you'll have plenty of time to nab them again."

He pursed his lips as he thought it over. "All right. You girls, go now. Moira, in the house."

"It's a lodge, and we don't wanna—"

"—go."

They folded their arms across their chests and stuck out their lower lips.

Louis pushed Katie in the direction of the ranch and said to Moira, "I think I have made a bargain." He followed her toward the door. "You better make the call. I really do not want to 'nab' them again. They are quite noisy for children."

"That's because they're normal. Not like we were."

"Speak for yourself."

She opened the front door and led the way in. Just before Louis closed it behind them, she peeked out and watched Katie and Nicole stroll down the road, their heads bent together in conversation. They were in no hurry at first, then suddenly hopped into a run, as if they couldn't wait to find their dad and tell him they'd discovered a real, live prince.

And finally proven "Chloe" to be a real, live princess in disguise.

Louis closed the door firmly, blocking Moira's view, and locked it. At twelve, when she'd been chauffeured away from her father's castle, bound for the United States, she'd felt just like Katie and Nicole seemed to feel. She'd been alternately dejected and excited.

She hadn't wanted to go at first, but her father had promised that American doctors were more capable of dealing with her dog-bite injury. Emma had made the prospect of living in a foreign country sound like an adventure, so she'd brightened up.

For the first time, Moira had an inkling of why her father had sent her away. He must have known she was in danger. Just as she wanted to keep Katie and Nicole safe from Louis, he'd wanted to keep her safe. He must have known someone was trying to harm her; he probably never suspected Louis.

Had he loved her after all? As much as she loved Katie and Nicole? If so, he'd undoubtedly suffered over his decision to send her away.

If only she'd known, she never would have traded places with Chloe. Now that he was dead, it really didn't matter anymore.

Katie and Nicole were out there, all alone on the mountain. They were so small; just two munchkins, as Dutch called them. She hoped that all the days they'd played in the mountains would stand them in good stead until they were back with Dutch or MaryAnne.

As worried as she was about them, she wasn't nearly as scared as she would be if they were anywhere near Louis. She felt like a parent.

Finally she felt very close to her father.

DUTCH MADE RECORD TIME on the drive from the airport to the ranch, hoping Chloe hadn't gotten on the plane, hoping she'd just returned Friday to her owner, hoping she'd be waiting for him. If she hadn't seen him, she wouldn't even know he'd followed her. She wouldn't know he'd seen the royal jet, that he'd put two and two together and figured out just whom she'd traded places with.

He poked his head into the office. "You seen Chloe?"

MaryAnne, registering guests who'd arrived by car, turned to him and took too long to answer, in his opinion. "Chloe?" She shook her head. "No, I don't—"

"Thanks," he barked on his way out the door.

Please let her be here.

He ducked his head into every doorway en route to the girls' dorm, asked everyone he bumped into if they'd seen her. He barged into her room without knocking. It was its usual mess, as if she didn't know how to make a bed or pick up her own clothes.

His laugh was short, and definitely not sweet. Of course she didn't know how to make a bed or pick up after herself. She'd been born a princess. She'd always had servants do the drudge work for her. What the heck was she thinking, trading places with Chloe Marshall?

What did she want?

He sank onto the edge of her bunk, rested his elbows on his knees and gave the matter some deep thought. If she'd been Chloe, he could have shown her how much he loved her by giving her the moon. But dammit, she was a royal princess who'd always had the best of everything. What could he possibly give her?

He looked around at all her stuff. Had she gotten on the plane or was she coming back to pack? Or would she just buy everything new and start over?

Sitting there for ten years wouldn't help him figure her out. He kicked a path through the clutter on the floor and left the dorm.

"Hey, boss," Wade said on his way through the square.

"Wade…"

"Yeah, boss?"

"You seen Chloe?"

"She left with Luiz."

Now there was an answer Dutch hadn't expected. "Luiz?"

"Yeah. They were in your Jeep. I figured you knew."

MaryAnne stepped out onto the porch in front of the office and hollered, "Dutch, phone call!"

He waved to let her know he'd heard, but he wasn't ready to let Wade go yet. "They say where they were going?"

Wade shook his head and shrugged. "Nope. Just headed straight on outta here."

MaryAnne hollered again, "Dutch, Chloe's on the phone."

He took off running, charged through the office without acknowledging anyone or anything in his way. "Chloe?" he barked into the receiver.

"Dutch."

"Where are you?"

"I'm at your lod— Ow. Cut it out."

He heard scuffling. Yes, that's what it was.

"I guess I can't say right now."

"What the hell's going on?"

"I'm supposed to give you a message. Katie and Nicole are fine right now."

He glanced around the office, surprised they weren't with MaryAnne. They always liked to help her check in the new guests. "Where're the girls?"

"It was slow. They went out to play for a while."

Into the phone, he barked, "Where are they?"

"They're walking down the ro— Ow." More sounds of scuffling. "I said cut it out, you lowlife."

A slap then. A definite slap.

"Okay, okay, I'm getting to it. Dutch, are you still there?"

"Where the hell else would I be?" he roared. "What's going on? Is Luiz with you?"

"Uh, yeah."

"Are you up at my lodge?"

"Uh-huh."

"Katie and Nicole are with you?"

"No."

Another slap, a man's growled order.

"Butt face" was her response to that. "Okay, Dutch, here's what I'm supposed to tell you. You're supposed to bring half a million dollars..." Her voice faded slightly as she said, "That *is* five hundred thousand, you moron."

Dutch figured Luiz either hadn't been in this country long enough to learn details or didn't have too many brains, which scared him just as much as if the guy were smart.

"Anyway, five hundred thousand dollars. I can't tell you where until I call you back and see if you have it."

"Tell him I have it."

She didn't answer immediately. "Yeah, I know it'll take you a while to get it together."

He wanted to get her back right away, and she was stalling? "I can be there whenever you say."

"After you get the girls back? They're on their way down—"

The connection ended.

MaryAnne was hanging on his arm. "Dutch, is everything all right? Where are Katie and Nicole?"

"If I understood correctly, I think they're on the road coming back from my lodge."

"What's going on?"

"I think Chloe's been kidnapped." If swapping places with the real Chloe had been a game to her, was this?

"You *think?*"

"Well, it's either that or she's out for my money." If he paid the ransom, would she leave?

It doesn't matter. Not that he wanted her to leave, but he loved her. If he could buy her freedom, he would. No strings attached.

MaryAnne jabbed her finger in his chest. Hard. "Don't be ridiculous. Money doesn't matter to Chloe."

He cocked his head on an angle for a better look at his sister. "How do you know?"

She snorted. "She's almost thirty and she'd rather stay in the dorm than let you 'take care of her,' that's how."

"Well, if that phone call was on the level, she needs me now."

MOIRA'S BIGGEST FEAR was that her life was about to be snuffed out, and she hadn't had the nerve to tell

Dutch how much she loved him. She'd stopped him from telling her, when now she'd give anything to hear him say, "I love you."

Would it be "I love you, Chloe" or "I love you, Moira?" Because as soon as he picked up Katie and Nicole—she was pretty sure she'd given him enough clues as to where they were—he'd know the truth. They'd tell him everything they'd heard and learned.

More than she'd been willing to tell him, which he probably would consider a lie of omission.

She was sorry Katie and Nicole knew, because now Chloe's future was at risk. She was glad Dutch knew, because now there'd be no more secrets—if he'd even have anything to do with her again.

If she lived that long. Louis had dragged Moira from room to room throughout the lodge until he turned up a handgun and two rifles, with which he quickly acquainted himself.

After Dutch picked up Katie and Nicole, would he come for her? It was Sunday. The banks were closed. No one in their right mind kept half a million dollars in cash laying around, even if they were as proud of everything they'd accumulated as Dutch was. As much as he liked to share what he had, she could never pay him back if he did this for her.

But he'd said he'd come whenever she told him to.

Waiting was hard enough without having to do it in Dutch's lodge, every inch of which reminded her of him. Being there again magnified her hurt, her fear. All she'd wanted was a normal, average life. She'd come so close in this lodge. In his bedroom. In Dutch's strong, loving arms.

She didn't want to die under his roof.

When she thought Katie and Nicole had been gone long enough to get to safety, she turned to her brother and baited him. "Dutch isn't coming, you know. He won't pay you a dime for me."

Louis's laugh showed he couldn't have cared less. "I do not want his money."

He quit laughing, which was even worse and gave her goose bumps.

"Do not misunderstand, Moira. If he brings it, I will take it. But that is not why I am here."

"Then why?"

"You took my throne."

"It wasn't yours—"

"I will take your lover."

"Don't be absurd. He's just my boss."

"You do not be absurd. I saw you together. If he is not your lover yet, he wants to be."

"No, you're wrong. I mean nothing to him. He cares only for his ranch."

He laughed again. "You work too hard to protect him, I think."

She shook her head and tried to look unimpressed. She had to succeed at this ruse. After all, if he killed Dutch instead of her, what would she have to live for? A lifetime of guilt and regret?

He aimed the handgun at her. "Come. There is more to prepare."

"What?"

"I need—what do you say?—gasoline."

NEVER IN HIS WILDEST DREAMS did Dutch think he'd ever meet a princess, let alone play her knight in shining armor. Nor did he ever think he'd be called on to give up what he'd worked for, what he'd earned. And he'd be damned if he'd do it without getting Chloe back in one piece, safe and sound. After all, she was the woman he wanted by his side for the rest of his life.

But first he had to make sense of Katie and Nicole's wild, excited chatter while they stood in the middle of the road to his lodge.

"You're sure you're all right?" He couldn't get them to stand still long enough to check for blood or bruises.

"Daddy, Daddy—"

"—she's a princess."

"Uh-huh. Hold still."

"And her brother's a prince, only not a very nice—"

"—one. He was mean."

"Did he hurt you?"

"He tied us up and put bandannas in our—"

"—mouths, but he hit Chloe. I mean Moira."

Which Chloe had that bastard hit? Dutch still didn't know for sure.

MaryAnne splayed her hands on her hips. She shook her head. "Girls, you know you have to tell the truth."

"But we are! Chloe's really Princess Moira, and the evil prince—"

"—captured her."

MaryAnne tsked at them. "I think we're going to have to take some of your storybooks away for a while."

"It's true. We put our—"

"—peas under her sleeping bag, 'n' she couldn't sleep."

"Now, Katie—"

Dutch's hand whipped up to stop them all. Having information that MaryAnne didn't already have, he studied his girls intently. "You say Chloe's really Moira?"

They nodded so hard, they should have been dizzy.

"That's what we've been tryin' to—"

"—tell you."

"Who's Moira?" MaryAnne asked.

"She's a princess—"

"—from Ennsway."

"Uh-huh." She shook her head at Dutch. "Don't tell me you're buying this."

He rubbed the back of his neck. "Well..."

"Dutch, I'm surprised at you. Chloe Marshall is just who she says she is—a cowgirl from Texas, a rodeo trick rider, a... a... Well, whatever she says she is."

"The thing is, MaryAnne, she told me yesterday that she's not really Chloe. So, I gotta go with what Katie and Nicole are telling me now. Only I'm not sure who—"

"She *told* you she's not Chloe?" MaryAnne sagged against the fender of her truck.

He nodded. "I'm going up to the lodge. You take the girls back with you, okay? And don't let them talk to anyone."

"Look out for Prince Louis, Daddy. He's—"

"—mean."

"Is he armed?" MaryAnne asked.

"Doesn't matter," Dutch responded. "If he wasn't before, he will be by the time I get there."

ROCKS CRUNCHED beneath the tires as Dutch skidded his truck to a stop. Keeping the door between him and the lodge, he eased out.

"Chloe!"

The front door opened. Chloe, wearing the same tight, dyed tank top that she'd had on earlier, stepped onto the porch.

It must be her.

Luiz followed, a rifle in his hand, the barrel resting oh-so-casually against his shoulder. "My sister is fine, *boss.*"

"A man doesn't treat his sister like trade goods, Luiz. You all right, Chloe?"

Her nod was short and jerky, as Luiz had a hold of her by her hair. Dutch craved the sound of her voice.

Luiz waved the rifle. "Step away from the truck, *boss*. And keep your hands where I can see them."

"No, Dutch, don't do it. Get back in the—" Her whole body twisted as Luiz shook her, like a terrier does a rat. "Don't come any close—"

Dutch's heart caught in his throat. He'd sign over his whole ranch in a second if Luiz would just let her go.

She fell to her knees, then tried to bite Luiz right above his knee, but he was too quick for her and jerked her head away from her target.

Dutch stepped away from the shield of the truck's door. "Chloe, don't—"

"Her name is Moira. Formerly Her Royal Highness and Princess of Ennsway." Luiz squinted at him and demanded, "Where is the money?"

Dutch thumbed over his shoulder. "In a bag on the seat."

"Get it. Slowly. Throw it over to the Jeep, then walk toward me."

Dutch had brought a leather carry-on bag stuffed with newspaper and topped off with hundred-dollar bills—all he had on hand. He managed to reach in and grab it without turning and showing off the handgun stuffed in the waistband in back of his jeans.

"I always thought you royal people were different than everyone else."

Luiz—*this guy's a prince?*—laughed. "Oh, but we are."

Dutch shook his head, holding Luiz's gaze all the while. "No, you're not." He tossed the bag toward the Jeep. It landed with a nice, heavy thud that spoke of quick cash.

"Come this way. Slowly. And do not try anything."

Dutch did so, his hands on his hips so he could reach the gun faster—when the time was right. "You're no different than a common, ordinary thug. A lowlife who uses women and children to take what isn't his."

"And what of my sister who took what was not hers to take?"

"Oh, give it a rest," Chloe snapped.

"Shut up."

Dutch locked gazes with her. With the barest lift of his chin, he tried to tell her to get to her feet. Only then could she run if she got the chance. If he could give it to her.

"He's not interested in what you think I did to you," she said as she got one foot beneath her, then the other.

"Shut up!"

"You've got the money," Dutch interrupted impatiently. Leave it to Chloe to talk herself in deeper when he was doing his best to get her away from Luiz before she got hurt. At least that left no doubt she was *his* Chloe. "Take the Jeep and go."

"He doesn't want the money, Dutch."

He played every card he had to distract the creep. "Half a million dollars? Oh, I don't know, Chloe. It's a rare man that can pass that up."

"You're right," Luiz said. "But first, the grand finale." He flicked open a gold lighter and ignited it, then tossed it through the front door.

Flames torched up the foyer, licking the dark oak door, turning it black. Luiz, dragging Chloe along as a shield, keeping her too close for Dutch to risk a shot, inched toward the Jeep.

Suddenly, Dutch's lodge meant nothing to him. Not without Chloe to make it a home.

She kicked backward at his legs, but wasn't able to make good, hard contact. "You're a no-good excuse for a human being, you know that, Louis?"

He laughed and paused beside the leather bag. "Pick it up."

"Pick it up yourself."

"I would, but my hands are busy."

"Use your feet, you baboon," she snapped.

He shook her by the hair again.

"Go ahead, pull my hair out. I still won't pick it up."

"Bah!" He shoved her facedown into the dirt and scooped up the bag.

As Luiz bolted for the Jeep, Dutch's instincts sent him sprinting toward Chloe.

She spit out dirt. "Stay back!"

Luiz darted behind the steering wheel and aimed the rifle in their direction. "You should listen to her." He leveled it at Dutch's chest.

Chloe surged to her feet and flung herself in front of Dutch, facing her brother. "You've got the money. You're burning his house down. Go!"

With Chloe in the way of a bullet that could come any second, Dutch would have sworn his heart stopped right then. Though she fought to stay in front in harm's way, he strong-armed her behind him. He couldn't control her long enough to get his own gun out, though. "Stay there, dammit."

She ducked around him until she was in front again.

"Move, Moira. I want his life."

"Then you'll have to kill me first."

The tip of the rifle wavered.

Dutch swung her around behind him again. "Stay there, dammit, or I'll knock you out myself."

She dodged between them again, out of Dutch's grasp. He reached behind him and grabbed his gun. Luiz glared at her, then spat into the dust. He started the engine and, with a lurch to the right, he swerved the Jeep away from them, away from the lodge.

Dutch took aim. "Is he really your brother?"

"Yes."

He lowered his arm.

"Don't let that stop you!"

He shook his head. "He didn't hurt anyone."

"Spineless weasel."

He wasn't sure if she was referring to her brother, or to him because he wouldn't take a shot at his own Jeep. It didn't matter, though, because in another second, she'd walked right into his arms. With her pressed against his chest, what else was there for him to care about at the moment?

"I meant him," she said.

He chuckled.

"Ohmigod, your lodge!"

He didn't have to turn to see it. He could hear the flames engulf the wood, eat everything but the clothes on his back, swallow what he used to think was important.

She struggled in his arms. "We have to do something."

"It'll be gone before anyone can get here."

"But, Dutch—"

He held her at arm's length and shook her lightly. "Are you always so damned impulsive?"

When she looked up at him and opened her mouth to answer—and probably a tart reply, at that—he tugged her to him again, tilted his head and closed his lips over hers.

She tasted of dirt, of salt and sweat, and sweeter than anything in his life. Unable to get enough of her, he blazed a trail of kisses up to her temple.

"I'm sorry about your lodge," she whispered softly, as if she couldn't find her breath.

"It doesn't matter."

"It does."

He continued his trail across her eyelids. "No, not without you."

"I know how much you love your lodge and your ranch."

"I love you." He framed her head tenderly between his hands and wandered into delicate territory beneath her ear, down her neck. "Besides, it's probably karma."

After a moment, she asked, "What is?"

He released her from his lips, but couldn't bear to take his hands off her. "I got it by a lie. I guess it's karma that I lose it the same way."

"But you didn't lie. I did."

He shrugged. "This time."

"Wait a minute. You told a lie?"

He grimaced and nodded, and turned to watch his lodge burn down, grateful there was no wind to carry flames to the forest.

"Tell me."

"Nope."

"Trust me, it'll feel good to get it off your chest." He cocked his head at her.

"I should know."

He summoned up his nerve and squared his shoulders. "I told a man I rode bulls."

She blinked up at him.

"You don't understand."

"No kidding, Sherlock."

He remembered it as if it were yesterday. "I wanted that movie role more than anything I'd ever wanted in my whole life. I wanted the money, the prestige, Hollywood, everything. I wanted what I could buy with that money—this ranch. You're nodding."

"Grass is greener. Been there, done that."

"Look, if I'm going to bare my soul here, do you think you could let me get through it?"

"Sorry." Her smile said she wasn't. "Go on."

"Where was I? Oh, yeah. But the director asked me if I'd ever ridden bulls, and I knew if I told the truth, I'd get the old 'don't call us, we'll call you' routine. So I said yes."

She shook her head at him, and he didn't think she was taking him very seriously.

"And that's the only lie you ever told in your entire life?"

"Yep."

She stared up at him as if he had two heads.

"He put me on a bull that afternoon, too."

Laughter bubbled from her. "Now that's karma." She sobered and gestured toward his blackening lodge. "Not this. This is my fault."

"It's just a thing. Don't worry about it."

She waved her hand in front of his face. "Hello? Who are you and what have you done with Dutch?"

He grabbed her hand and kissed her knuckles. "I'm not going anywhere, darlin'. What about you?"

"I love you. I know that doesn't make up for your home—"

"We'll rebuild."

"But you're going to Hollywood, remember?"

"Come with me."

"I can't."

He studied her eyes, saw determination there and then understood. "Too many photographers, right?"

"One is too many."

"Yeah, I've seen how you treat them. We'll figure something out."

OFFICER CARLSON arrived in response to Dutch's cell call. "Fire department's on its way."

Moira looked at what remained of the lodge and knew Dutch had been right when he'd said no one could get there in time. The fire department would be a formality to make sure the fire was out, to keep it from sparking up later and spreading.

"Anybody hurt?"

"Nope," Dutch answered.

Carlson shook his head. "Man, Mr. Cordwin, your lodge and your Jeep both in one day."

"My Jeep?"

"His Jeep?"

"Yeah, I saw what was left of it at the bottom of a ravine. Paramedics are on their way down now, but it's too late. Have any idea who it was?"

Moira glanced at Dutch.

He shook his head. "Just hired him a few days ago. Went by the name of Luiz."

Carlson returned to his vehicle to respond to a call.

"You just lied for me, Dutch."

"Yep." He tightened his arm around her. "I reckon, since I want to keep you around, I might have to do a bit of that. To Katie and Nicole, for starters."

She rested her head on his chest and relished the security she felt in his arms.

"In case I didn't say it before, I love you, Chloe."

He said it. She snuggled closer.

"How do you feel about changing your name again?" He slipped his fingers beneath her chin and tipped her face up to his. "I was thinkin' Chloe Cordwin has a nice ring to it. Got anyone you want to invite to a wedding?"

She framed his face with her hands, holding more than she'd ever dreamed at her fingertips.

"Just you."

Epilogue

"Mail's here," Dutch announced. "Special delivery from Baesland-Ennsway."

"Oh, good." Moira dried her hands on a kitchen towel.

"Where're the girls?"

"Katie's watching a tape on trick riding, and Nicole's trying on her new jods."

"Amazing how they're turning into two separate people, isn't it?"

She held out her hand. "Don't change the subject."

He started to hand the large envelope to her, then snapped it back against his chest. "It came by courier."

"Really?" She couldn't imagine what warranted that. "Ooh, let me have it. Quick."

His eyebrows rose. When she reached for it, he held it over his head, making her laugh.

"Come on, Dutch, hand it over."

"Can't."

"Why not?"

"It's for me."

"Yeah, right. Why would she write to you?"

"I don't know." He appeared to give the matter a

great deal of thought, which earned him a punch in the arm. "Okay, let's see." He unzipped the cardboard, having to continually dodge Moira's grasps as he did so. Inside was another envelope. "Wow, wax on the back and everything."

"Jeez, Dutch, that's the royal seal."

"She never sent you anything like this."

"Careful, I might think you like my knowing a queen."

He popped the wax, opened the envelope and peeked in. "It's not from her. It's from William. Some kind of award."

"Oh, God." She groaned. *Please don't let it be a dukedom.* She'd come all this way, chasing her own grass-is-greener ghosts. She'd found that, for her, anonymity *was* what she truly wanted. Becoming a duchess would be awful.

She sank into the nearest chair. Absently she twisted her strand of pearls. Chloe wouldn't let William do this to her, would she?

"Sir Dutch Cordwin. Hey, I've been knighted for chivalry."

She sighed with relief. "Well, you deserve it."

"Scared you, though, didn't it?"

"What're you grinning about? You're the one who hates royalty."

"Well, that was before I got to know one." He hunkered down beside her and rested his hand on her expanding belly. "Or two."

"Wrong on both counts, cowboy. Now put that mail away before Katie and Nicole see it."

"You *still* think they're convinced we made the story up to appease a crazy man?"

Who could trust nine-year-olds to keep a secret like hers? "I do."

"Then how come every time you serve peas for dinner, I have to scoop them out from under the mattress in the morning?"

"Because I burn them?"

He chuckled, and wrapped her more snugly in his arms. "Well, maybe. So I'm a knight, and you're still happy being a rancher's wife?"

She threaded her fingers through his dark hair and tugged on it playfully. "Yes, but just so you don't go getting cocky, there's more to my life than that. I'm Katie and Nicole's stepmom, and my best friend happens to be my sister-in-law."

He snapped his fingers. "That reminds me. MaryAnne wants to know if she can bring Ben to supper."

"Sure, I'll just throw in another pizza."

He grimaced. "I'll cook tonight, okay, princess? You can scoop ice cream for dessert. What kind do we have this week?"

"Fantastic Fantasy Fudge."

"Again?"

She gazed into his eyes, something she never tired of. And not because they were the same, rich color as fudge. "It reminds me of your eyes." She leaned forward and gave him a kiss hot enough to melt a whole gallon of ice cream. "It reminds me of you."

"You say the girls are busy?"

"Mmm-hmm."

"How 'bout a little afternoon delight with a knight?"

"Sounds even better than ice cream. When are Ben and MaryAnne due?"

"Soon." He grabbed her hand and headed for the stairs. "But not too soon."

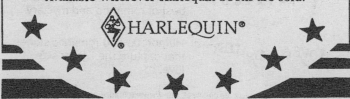

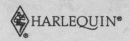

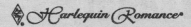

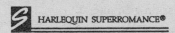

DEBBIE MACOMBER

invites you to the

HEART OF TEXAS

Join Debbie Macomber as she brings you the lives and loves of the folks in the ranching community of Promise, Texas.

If you loved Midnight Sons—don't miss Heart of Texas! A brand-new six-book series from Debbie Macomber.

Available in February 1998 at your favorite retail store.

Heart of Texas by Debbie Macomber

Lonesome Cowboy	February '98
Texas Two-Step	March '98
Caroline's Child	April '98
Dr. Texas	May '98
Nell's Cowboy	June '98
Lone Star Baby	July '98

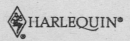

HARLEQUIN®

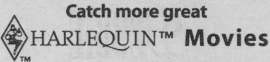

MEN at WORK

All work and no play? Not these men!

April 1998

KNIGHT SPARKS by Mary Lynn Baxter

Sexy lawman Rance Knight made a career of arresting the bad guys. Somehow, though, he thought policewoman Carly Mitchum was framed. Once they'd uncovered the truth, could Rance let Carly go...or would he make a citizen's arrest?

May 1998

HOODWINKED by Diana Palmer

CEO Jake Edwards donned coveralls and went undercover as a mechanic to find the saboteur in his company. Nothing—or no one—would distract him, not even beautiful secretary Maureen Harris. Jake had to catch the thief—*and* the woman who'd stolen his heart!

June 1998

DEFYING GRAVITY by Rachel Lee

Tim O'Shaughnessy and his business partner, Liz Pennington, had always been close—but never *this* close. As the danger of their assignment escalated, so did their passion. When the job was over, could they ever go back to business as usual?

MEN AT WORK™

Available at your favorite retail outlet!

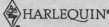 

Look us up on-line at: http://www.romance.net   PMAW1